ONLY EVER YOU

WILD FIRE SERIES

J.H. CROIX

For trying to stay true to yourself even when it feels like maybe you aren't what the world expects.

Chapter One

LUNA TALTON

A gust of salty air blew my hair wild. I lifted a hand to catch it and smooth it back. I looked out over the water, marveling at the view. The mountains towered in the distance and the sun struck sparks off the ocean's surface. Even though I'd grown up in Alaska, it never failed to wow me. Whenever people told me they didn't believe in any kind of spirituality, I would tell them they just needed to go to Alaska. Because it was truly a spiritual experience. Nature here snatched your breath right out of your lungs and reminded you that the whole world was a cathedral.

"Luna!" My friend Casey's voice reached me and I spun around.

She was lugging a cooler all by herself and stumbled a little on the rock-strewn shoreline. I hurried over and reached for the other handle. "What's in here?" I asked.

"Food," she teased. "We have empty coolers too. Everyone tells me we have fish to catch. Have you ever done this?" she asked me as her gaze whisked over to several fishing nets propped up against another cooler nearby on the beach.

"Of course! Dipnetting is an Alaskan tradition. If you grow up here, you have to do it. I can't even imagine not doing it."

After we set the cooler down, I opened it to peer inside. "Oh wow, you didn't mess around." When I glanced up at Casey, she grinned. "Well, you said we might be here all day."

Someone called her name. She looked over her shoulder, a smile stretching across her face. Her cheeks went pink when I chimed in, "You are so in love."

She shrugged. "I am. And, it's really the best thing ever."

I impulsively hugged her. "Everyone deserves love like what you and Leo have," I said just before her fiancé reached us.

"Hey, Luna," Leo said, stopping beside us. "Ready to net some salmon?"

"Absolutely!"

Leo chuckled, holding two fishing nets aloft. "I have two options for nets. There's my favorite, which is the cedar handle. I also brought a stainless steel one."

Casey studied the nets before her gaze bounced to me. "People are *really* into the nets for this. I can't dipnet yet. I haven't been here a full year yet."

"You can watch. It's fun," I replied.

I glanced around the area. Seagulls were calling raucously in the air, and I could hear the distant screech of an eagle. We were at the Kenai River in Alaska, a favorite destination for dipnetting. The activity was aptly named. You gathered on the shoreline at the edge of the water with handheld fishing nets to catch the salmon swimming upriver. Some people chose to dipnet with nets dangling over the edge of boats, but I'd always preferred to be on the shoreline. We were near the mouth of the river, where the fish came rushing in from the ocean in a race to spawn before they died. If they didn't get scooped up in a net, they would spawn and die.

The beach was getting crowded. There were regulations for the size of the nets and just about everyone had an opinion on the best nets.

I started to suit up in my neoprene fishing waders. Casey looked around, commenting, "This is crazy!"

"What do you mean?" I asked as I stepped into my wading boots.

"You and Leo told me about it, and Maisie was telling me—" Casey turned away as Maisie called out a greeting. We waved back and Casey continued, "I guess I didn't realize there would be this many people. Parking is practically a competitive sport."

I grinned. "It's awesome. Fun though it is, it's serious. People rely on the salmon they catch here to feed their families. One person can get up to twenty-five salmon with an additional ten salmon for each family member. That's a lot of food. Not to mention how fresh Alaskan silver salmon is." I tapped my fingers together in the motion for a chef's kiss.

Maisie reached us with Amelia, Lucy, Tish, Griffin, and more trailing behind her. Recently, I'd started to feel like the odd one out. Many of my friends were happily married or coupled up, and I was still very single. I couldn't even imagine being anything but single.

"Hey, Parker," Griffin called.

My eyes instantly swung in his direction, while I ordered my hormones to ignore Parker Reeves. I also studiously ignored the inconvenient embarrassment that he didn't recognize me. *It was ten years ago. Forget about it.*

"Hey, hey," Parker said with a lopsided grin when he stopped by our group.

"Is this your first year dipnetting?" Casey asked him.

Parker shook his head. "No, ma'am," he teased.

"I might have only moved to Willow Brook in the last year, but I am a born and bred Alaskan."

"Well, I'm gonna watch and learn. Show me your net," Casey said.

Beck stopped beside Maisie. "That sounds a little inappropriate, Casey," he teased with an exaggerated brow waggle.

Casey rolled her eyes. "Look, this is my first time watching this. Everybody keeps talking about their nets, so I'm trying to understand why they're so important."

Parker's grin sent sparks pinwheeling inside of me. "A lot of people build their own nets." He gestured to the net I was holding. "I'm on team-Luna. I like them with a cedar handle and a rectangular net. The cedar floats in the water, so it makes those easy to hold."

Casey nodded along. "Hmm. I guess I have until next year to figure out what kind of net I want."

The beach was getting more and more crowded. Amelia caught my eye. "I like the cedar handle too because it floats."

Beck chimed in, "Well, now there are advantages to the stainless-steel ones because your grip slides more easily if you need to adjust it."

"You undercut your own point. If your hands can slide easier, you can lose your grip," Maisie pointed out. Maisie stopped beside Casey, pulling her into a side hug. "I was new at this too, but I've done it for a few years now and it's really fun. You're gonna love it when you get to go next year."

"I sure love salmon, so I'm looking forward to it." She glanced toward me, worry creasing her brow. "I can eat the salmon Leo catches, right?"

I burst out laughing. "Of course, you just have to officially be a resident before you can get a dipnetting permit."

"Too bad we can't keep any king salmon," Amelia commented.

I nodded when I glanced her way. "I know. I remember when it was a big deal to catch them dipnetting. Here's hoping the numbers improve again."

It wasn't long before we were all wading into the ocean. I tended to push the envelope on this and go as far out as I could. I loved the feeling of the water rushing against me. Today, the fish were coming in fast and I could feel them bouncing against my legs. I had almost caught my limit when I waded back into the water to try to catch one more salmon.

The sun was high in the sky, and the wind was starting to pick up so the water was getting choppy. I didn't think much of it when a boat came rolling down the river. The boat's wake was high enough that my feet lifted off the sandy bottom. I still didn't worry until several minutes ticked by and I realized I was drifting further away from the shoreline.

"Luna!"

I recognized Beck's voice and glanced back. "Yeah?"

"You okay?"

I wanted to tell him I was completely fine. I was independent, some people would probably think I was stubbornly so. I hated asking for help. Ever. But I didn't want to be stupid and I was deeply practical. I knew that if I didn't somehow change course, I might start drifting too far out into the current where the water could carry me out to sea. Literally.

The water was also cold. Alaska wasn't a place where people swam without a wetsuit, even on the hottest days of summer. That cold water was beginning to seep over the tops of my waders. I was smart though, and I was wearing a life jacket.

I glanced back at Beck and called out, "I'm not sure!"

I turned to face the shore so I could keep an eye on how fast I might be drifting away. I wasn't alone in this predicament. I could see another person, maybe fifty feet away, who was trying to swim directly back to shore. I knew that wasn't the best move. It was safer to swim at an angle across the current.

I was a strong swimmer, but I had a fishing net in hand and was wearing waders that were starting to fill with water. I did the only practical thing I could do. I kept a hold of the net because it was floating, but I began to kick with my feet and unbuckle the tops of my wader straps. After I got them off, I turned them upside down so the water drained out and hooked the boots under my armpits. When I glanced toward the shoreline again, I noticed it was further away.

There were voices calling to those of us who had gotten swept away due to the boat's wake.

"Don't panic, Luna," I said to myself. "You're going to be fine."

I was starting to shiver. I kept my eyes on the shore and began to swim, letting go of my net finally. Only a moment later as I was starting to despair, a small boat approached and someone called my name.

When I looked over, I saw Parker and Griffin in the boat. Parker caught my eye. "We're cutting the engine and I'm going to get you out of there."

Parker slowly reached a hand out, saying, "Just grab my hand, Luna. I've got you."

Cold as I was, my hands felt numb so it was difficult to hold on. Parker's grip was strong and he kept a firm hold on me as he reached for my other arm. He lifted me into the boat, scooping me in his strong arms. I didn't realize my teeth were chattering until I tried to talk.

"I didn't kn-kn-kn-know..."

"Wait to talk," Parker said. He held me in his protective embrace.

With it being so crowded and busy, I couldn't

even remember when I'd last seen him on the beach. He was in jeans and a T-shirt. I savored the feel of his warmth. Griffin leaned into the water to get my net and tossed it over the side of the boat. I glanced over to see another boat had gone to rescue the two other people who had drifted out.

"All right, I'm headed to shore," Griffin said.

"You have any blankets on board?" Parker asked.

Griffin pointed to a seat. Parker kept an arm around me as he leaned over and opened it to pull out a big blanket. A moment later, he wrapped it around me.

"You don't have to keep holding me," I finally managed when I could catch my breath.

When he glanced down and my eyes locked with his, everything felt suspended. My heart thumped hard against my ribs, the beat of it echoing. It was as if a pebble of fire dropped into a pond and rippled through me. I became acutely aware of the feeling of his palm curled on the edge of my hip.

"We need to get you warm," he said.

Chapter Two

PARKER REEVES

Luna blinked up at me. Her big blue eyes were wide and her dark curls were pulled up in a ponytail. Her teeth were still chattering when she replied, "I-I-I…"

She clenched her jaw, shaking her head as if in annoyance with herself for being cold. "I'm fine," she ground out through clenched teeth.

"Luna, that water isn't much above fifty degrees. A quick way to get hypothermia is to swim in the ocean in Alaska in the summer. It's pretty efficient," I said dryly.

I reached for the towel I'd gotten with the blanket and handed it to her. She dabbed at her face with it before almost burrowing into herself. "You might have a point," she said a moment later.

Her teeth had stopped chattering, but she was still shivering. "It was that boat wake," she said.

"Yeah, three people got carried out. How many fish did you get so far?"

"Twenty-four. I should've stopped."

I chuckled when I looked down at her again. Her shivering was slowing. At that moment, my heart gave a resounding kick and awareness struck me like a fiery bolt.

Luna was curled against me in a soft bundle. I wanted to hold her close, to protect her.

You want to do a lot more than protect her, my cynical mind chimed in.

Luna was cute, sexy, and downright delectable. I saw her just frequently enough that I had to make an effort not to notice her. She baked donuts for the local coffee shop, and she was friends with almost everybody I worked with. There was also something familiar about her. She reminded me of someone I'd met once. Just once, but the memory shined bright. Yet, Luna had crazy wild curls, while that someone had stick straight hair and a different name. I told myself again that it was just a fluke.

"Do you want to drop your net in now and catch one more?" I managed to ask.

She glanced around. "How far until we get to the boat ramp?"

Griffin glanced over. "A few minutes. How are you doing?" he called over the sound of the motor.

"Getting warmer."

"We need to get you some dry clothes," I commented.

Luna let out a little sigh. "When I was little, my mom always used to tell me that I shouldn't go too far out. Lesson learned." She rolled her eyes.

I chuckled. "Nobody was gonna let you drift out to sea."

"Thank you very much for stopping. You were on the beach earlier. When did you decide to go out in a boat?"

"Well, it was pretty crowded and Griffin texted me that he had his boat, so I went over to meet him."

After a beat, she nodded. "You can't get swept away if you're in the boat."

"True," I agreed.

"I'm think I'm warm," she said.

"Would you like to keep the blanket?" I asked as I reluctantly eased my hold on her.

"Please. I'm still wet, so without it, I'll get cold fast."

"You didn't lose a thing," I pointed out, gesturing to the net and her waders. "Smart move to take those off."

She shrugged. "They were filling with water. I'm glad you all caught my net for me."

She let the blanket fall down around her waist before tucking the ends of it to hold it in place. My eyes dipped down to notice her T-shirt was damp. I forced my eyes back up before they lingered too long.

I cleared my throat before standing up and handing her the handle to her net. "Drop that in the water. You can get that last fish."

She tucked the handle to the net in a holder and let the net drag through the water by the boat. Minutes later, she let out a happy squeal when a fish swam into her net. She dragged it into the boat and started jumping up and down. "It's a king!

She quickly freed it from the net and held it up to show it off. Griffin threw a grin over his shoulder as he steered the boat toward the ramp.

When I looked over at Luna again, she was covered in sand with a few streaks of fish blood on her arms from a busy day of catching, gutting, and cleaning fish. Her curls blew in a wild riot around her shoulders, and all I could think was that I wanted her.

Chapter Three

LUNA

Months later

The trees rustled above as I stopped, resting my hands on my hips as I looked around. There was a distressed sounding animal nearby, but I didn't know what animal, or where it was. After I walked a little further, I came to an abrupt halt in front of a hole in the ground, almost a perfect square and maybe four feet deep. Inside, two moose calves looked up at me. I whipped my gaze in a circle to discover a mama moose lingering in the trees nearby.

At the moment, she was eyeing me cautiously, as if trying to decide if I was friend or foe. I'd grown up in Alaska, so I was deeply familiar with how protective moose were of their calves, rightly so. I needed to be careful.

"I'm going to help your babies!" I called over to her.

She remained in the edge of the trees, watching as I peered down at the moose calves. "Luna, what are you thinking?" I mused to myself.

My gaze flicked over my pink pajama bottoms with a fleece jacket thrown over the top. I'd heard the sounds while I was trying to enjoy my morning coffee. Worried, I'd decided to investigate. I quickly checked my pocket, pleased to discover I'd thought to grab my cell phone when I hurried out. I contemplated which of my friends might be awake at this hour and finally decided it was safe to text Casey.

Me: *I'm rescuing two moose calves. If I'm late to drop off the donuts, mama moose has probably trampled me.*

"There," I said to myself, or I suppose the moose.

I glanced around, considering my options. A few minutes later, I dragged two boards over from the shed nearby and made a little ramp. I brushed my hair out of my face and clambered down, knowing if I thought too much about it, I might talk myself out of it.

At this point, mama moose approached. "Don't you come down here," I warned her.

The moose calves were all legs. I'd guess they were maybe a few months old. For the second time this morning, I asked myself, "Luna, what are you thinking?"

Now, I was in this. I had to somehow get these two calves out of here. They were studying me with rapt curiosity.

"Well, I'm here," I announced.

I approached them, taking a herding approach to get one over toward the side of this hole where I lifted its front legs. The moose wiggled like crazy, and it was heavy enough I could barely hold on. I clumsily shoved the calf out from behind. "You made it!" I cheered when the calf scampered over to mama moose, who sniffed her all over.

I repeated the process with the other calf. This one was even more wiggly, giving me several kicks in the thighs with sharp hooves.

"Yay!" I cheered when calf two scrambled away from the edge of the hole.

I hoped mama moose had enough sense not to jump down in here, but I decided it was best to give her a few minutes to move away. My breath was heaving, and I was absolutely filthy. My pink flannel pajama top had a big tear in it. I was re-lieved I had a tank top on underneath. At least I wasn't flashing the wilderness in my backyard. All in all, I couldn't believe I'd gotten them out of here.

Peering out, I watched as the three moose walked a short distance and began snacking on some alder trees. It was early autumn in Alaska and chilly in the morning. That was Alaska.

"I'm going for it," I announced to them. Even mama moose ignored me.

I clambered back up my makeshift ramp and began running, only to hear mama moose following me. I didn't realize there was another human here until— "Ooof!"— I collided with someone.

I all but bounced off of this person's chest. It felt like the human equivalent of bumping into a rock wall. I stumbled and glanced up. "Parker?" I tried to catch my breath.

"Luna?"

I didn't have time to explain. "Hurry! There's a moose chasing me!"

Parker didn't seem to be in much of a hurry when I grabbed his arm and started dragging him.

"She's walking the other way now, Luna," he said, his tone super calm.

"Well, she was just chasing me." I dropped his arm, feeling sheepish.

"Yeah, I saw that."

"What are you doing here?" I finally thought to ask.

He thumbed over his shoulder. "Walking my dog."

A giant dog approached, loping along with his tongue hanging out and his tail wagging. "Oh," was all I could manage.

The dog approached me, his tail swishing against my legs. "What's his name?" I knelt down to greet the dog.

"Fuzzy," Parker said with a sheepish grin when I glanced up.

"Hey, Fuzzy." I scratched behind his ears, and he dipped his head down to press it into my chest, wiggling all over with pure joy.

A moment later, I straightened.

"I was walking up the trail and heard you cheering. Maybe I'm crazy, but I could've sworn you pushed one of those moose calves out of that hole over there." Parker gestured toward the square hole in the ground.

"You're not crazy." A laugh sputtered out. "That's exactly what I did. Both calves were in there, and that seemed like the only way to get them out."

Parker's low chuckle sent a sizzle of heat over my skin. I glanced around to see the moose were out of sight now. He walked over to peer inside the hole. "Could be a foundation for an old cabin." His gaze arced around the clearing. "Maybe somebody planned to build here and never did."

I shrugged. "I don't know."

When Parker looked back at me, I imagined I must've been quite the sight. His eyes dipped down before whipping back up. It was only then I recalled I had a big tear in my pajama top. My fitted tank top was the only thing protecting my bare skin from burning up under the heat of his gaze. I could've sworn my nipples perked in greeting.

"I should let you keep going," I said hurriedly.

My voice sounded breathless, which was annoying. Parker Reeves was cute with his shaggy dark blond hair and rich brown eyes. He had defined features with a bold nose and one of those jaws you could wax poetic about, all strong and chiseled. He tended to distract me, or rather, my hormones. If I had any effect on him, it was absolutely not obvious.

He nodded before asking, "Are you okay?"

My eyes dipped down, taking in the dirt smeared in streaks on my pajamas and jacket. "I'm fine."

Parker's lips quirked at the corners, his eyes sparking with a gleam that made my belly feel all tingly.

"Enjoy your hike!" I called as I began to make my exit, walking with my chin held high.

I blamed it entirely on Parker and his handsomeness that I promptly took three steps, tripped over a root, and fell flat on my face.

Chapter Four

PARKER

"Ooof!"

At the sound of her exclamation, I turned back to see Luna stumbling and falling to the ground. Fuzzy galloped over to her side, personally inspecting her with his nose.

A few strides later, I knelt down beside her. "Are you okay?"

Luna made a muffled sound before rolling over. Her already muddy shirt was even muddier now, along with her pajama bottoms. The streak of mud on her cheek was an endearing touch.

She let out a heavy sigh as she sat up. "I am fine. Oh, my God. I was just trying to have a quiet morning and have some coffee before I go back into the cafe to bake some donuts." Her nose wrinkled in annoyance.

"You've already been into town?" I glanced at my watch. "It's only six in the morning, Luna," I pointed out, trying to ignore how delectably cute she was.

She brushed her curls away from her forehead, tucking them behind her ears. The gesture hooked on the edge of my heart with its sweetness.

Her nose wrinkled as she looked up at me. "I'm a baker. Bakers bake early. I usually make the dough for the donuts at four. After that, I like to come back here and enjoy some coffee."

"Oh, that's right, you make the donuts," I said.

"I do." Her tone was pointed.

Straightening, I held a hand out. "Let's make sure you're all in one piece."

Luna sighed again, but she allowed me to help her up. I knew Luna in an acquaintance sort of way. I'd even scooped her out of the ocean when we happened to be dipnetting at the same time, and she drifted too far out. I saw her often at the coffee shop in downtown Willow Brook. Whether I knew her or not, it would've been difficult *not* to notice Luna. She was adorably pretty.

I tried not to notice that her tank top was now plastered to her skin, complete with mud smeared on it.

"Are you okay?" I asked again when she wobbled a little once she was fully on her feet.

She narrowed her eyes at me. "I'm fine." Before I could reply, she exclaimed, "Oh, no!"

Her face was getting paler by the second. Maybe I didn't know what was happening, but I was pretty sure she was about to faint. "How far away is your house?" I asked quickly.

"Just through the woods over there." She gestured to a narrow path through the trees. "I have tachycardia and I need my medication. I forgot all about it because of the moose and—" She wobbled again when she turned.

Leaning down, I scooped her up in my arms. I strode quickly down the short path. Although I'd gone hiking here with Fuzzy more than once, I'd never noticed the house. It was tucked in the trees, just enough out of sight to miss.

Moments later, we were in her kitchen. I waited while she took some medication.

"Do you need something else?" I asked.

She sat down at the kitchen table and gestured toward the sink. "Could you bring my water over?"

I quickly brought the glass over to her. She took a few swallows. I was unsure what to do and didn't feel comfortable leaving just yet. Meanwhile, Fuzzy had made himself at home. He plunked down on the kitchen floor right at Luna's feet, eyeing her with concern.

"Should I do anything?" I finally asked.

"You don't have to stay."

I studied her. Her skin was still pale. "I'm not leaving. Not yet."

Annoyance flickered in her eyes before she sighed. "In that case, you can have a seat, or maybe pour yourself some coffee," she offered.

"I'll take that coffee."

A few minutes later, the color had returned to her face. She looked mostly herself except for the mud on her face and clothes.

"Thank you for helping me this morning," she said, her smile sheepish.

I chuckled. "It's been a very Alaskan morning. By the way, this coffee is excellent."

She took a swallow of her water, adding, "Thank you for getting me home faster than I could've gotten myself here. Normally, I'm on top of my medication, but I lost track of time with the whole moose situation."

"I'm just glad you're okay."

"I have an issue with tachycardia," she explained. "I take beta blockers for it. Been dealing with it my whole life. It's not often that I forget something like that." She glanced down at Fuzzy. "Your dog is an absolute sweetheart." She nudged him with her foot, and he leaned over to nuzzle her calf.

I grinned. "He is the best boy. He seems to have decided he needs to stay close to you. I knew you made the donuts for Firehouse Cafe, but I had no idea you drove in at four in the morning to start."

She shrugged. "I love to bake, and it works for me. I'm up early anyway." Pausing, she glanced at her watch. "I'm going to need to get ready." She looked down at her muddy clothes. "It's been a *morning*," she finally said, her tone dry.

"Well, you have a story," I offered with a soft laugh.

Her responding giggle made my heartbeat kick a little faster. I finished off my coffee. "I'll get going. Where should I put my coffee mug?"

"Just leave it in the sink."

When I stood and walked over to the sink, Fuzzy didn't move. I turned back and gestured for him. "Come on, Fuzzy."

My dog looked up at Luna, as if trying to assess if it was safe for him to leave her side. After a few seconds, he reluctantly got up, heaving a dramatic sigh. "I'm pretty sure he'd prefer to stay with you."

Luna smiled as she swept her hand down his back. "Well, anytime you need a dog babysitter, just ask me."

"Be careful what you offer. I'm a hotshot firefighter. I fly out of town a lot," I teased.

Her eyes widened. "I'm serious! I love dogs."

"Well then, that's always good to know. As it is, I board him at the local kennel, or I find a friend to take care of him."

"Consider me your new kennel." She paused, her teeth catching her bottom lip. "I mean, if you want."

When I looked back at her, there were all kinds of things I wanted. Namely, to lace my fingers in her wild curls and kiss her. I kicked those thoughts to the curb. She'd just tripped and fallen in the forest after rescuing two moose calves and getting chased. The last thing she probably wanted was some guy kissing her.

With her cheeks pink and the smatter of freckles on her nose, it was difficult to keep my brain on track. "That's good to know, and I know where to find you now."

"You do. But I'm serious," she said earnestly as she stood from the table and approached me. "Let me give you my number, so you have it. Are you on Leo's crew?" At my nod, she continued, "I work with Casey, so she keeps me in the loop. Just text me, and Fuzzy can hang out here when you're out of town. It's perfect." She looked down at my dog. "Right, Fuzzy?"

As if he understood, he let out a soft woof and head-butted her hard enough to knock her over. Fortunately, she was standing beside the kitchen counter and easily caught her balance.

I recited my number, and she tapped it into her phone. A moment later, my phone vibrated with a text. *Luna Talton, dog sitter extraordinaire.*

I shook my head as I laughed. "Fuzzy's an easy dog, so anyone who knows him is usually willing to help, but it's nice to know you'd like to take care of him."

With that, I left, distracted enough by Luna that

I never did finish the hike I'd planned with Fuzzy. A few hours later when I was driving through town, my hands turned my steering wheel into the parking lot at Firehouse Café without me even thinking about it. As I approached the door, a sense of anticipation thrummed inside. I wondered if I would see Luna.

As the bell jingled on the door and I walked inside, Luna glanced up from where she was holding a tray of donuts as she placed them in the display case. My heart started drumming, hard and fast, against my rib cage.

Chapter Five

LUNA

The next morning

"What do you think?" Casey spun to face me, her ponytail bouncing with the motion.

I took a swallow from the frothy coffee drink she had just made me. "Mmmm. It's delicious. It's the perfect blend of coffee with the sweetness of chocolate and fruit. Honestly, I was a little skeptical when you told me you were making this," I told her.

"I hoped blackberry was subtle enough that it would give it a little zing." She looked so satisfied with herself that I snorted a laugh.

I took another swallow, letting out a happy sigh as I slipped my hips onto a stool in the kitchen at Firehouse Café. This was one of my favorite places to be and maybe my favorite part of the day. It was early in the morning and the café wasn't open yet.

This is when Casey and I, and anyone else who happened to be here, could chat while I baked donuts and she got things ready for the front. Sometimes Janet James, the owner, joined us, but more often than not it was just Casey and me with Josie occasionally here.

"How's Leo?" I asked when Casey sat down across from me at the wide table that ran through the center of the kitchen.

She sighed, her gaze a little dreamy. "He is so good, and so good to me." She shook her head, looking legitimately puzzled by this.

I slapped a hand on the table. "You deserve all the goodness life is bringing your way," I said firmly.

Casey's smile was soft as she looked over at me. "You're a good friend." She lifted her chin and nodded.

"Well, you are too," I pointed out.

The oven chimed, and I slipped off the stool to open it, quickly sliding out several trays of donuts. A moment later, they were cooling on the table while Casey was studying me. "You look like you're thinking really hard," I said, starting to feel a little squirrely inside.

"I *am* thinking."

"What about?"

"Well, you. You're always cheering everyone else on. You're so positive and optimistic, but you don't talk a lot about yourself. You talk about your baking and all that, and I know you have a cute little house. You come to card night, but—" She paused and shrugged. "I feel like there's a giant hole in your life story."

My heart stung a little. Sometimes, when it came to being a friend, I felt a little lost. Although I was born here and went to elementary school in Willow Brook, everything changed when I turned eight. My parents wanted to do the RV life and took me with them. I'd done online schooling and barely stayed anywhere long enough to make friends. I'd felt like a literal rolling stone. The one friend I thought I had turned out not to be much of a friend, but it took me a long time to figure that out.

Casey had been through her own challenges and had confided in me. Now, I felt like I'd let her down. I didn't even know how to explain what my experience was and why I struggled with it. I took an unsteady breath and told the truth as best I knew how. "My parents were RV influencers. They have an online channel and do the whole thing. I hated it, like *hated* it. They were part of the early wave when that kind of stuff was taking off online. They have millions of followers. They post stuff on there and travel. But when I was with them, the videos that got the most publicity, and therefore the ads, were ones that I was in. So, that was my life." My throat ached with the emotion I'd kept corked tightly inside.

It was difficult to explain how the pervasive loss of all privacy for so much of my late childhood and adolescence felt so traumatic.

"Ohhhh." Casey's mouth twisted to the side. "That doesn't sound great," she said slowly.

"It definitely wasn't great," I said earnestly. "My parents are still doing it, and they're disappointed that I refuse to be part of it anymore. Frankly, I'm surprised they haven't tried to adopt a kid just so they can produce more content." That last word—content—was laced with all the bitterness in my heart.

Casey was quiet for a few beats. When I met her gaze, sadness flickered in her eyes. "That sounds really shitty."

"It was—" I paused, pondering my words. "Lonely. I mean, all I knew was being with them in the camper and being on camera for everything. We were all over the Internet with cute little clips. There were tons of people commenting, but I—" I took a deep breath, letting it out in a soft sigh. "I didn't have any friends. We were always on the move, traveling all over Alaska. We drove down to the lower 48 every winter. I've never even had a boyfriend. My parents kept saying I had so many people who cared about me online, but they were just comments on posts, and that's not a friend."

Casey blinked. "Oh, Luna." She stood from the table and rounded it quickly, pulling me into a hug.

Casey gave great hugs. She squeezed tightly before stepping back. "You have friends now. Everyone loves you here. And, you need to go on a date! It doesn't have to be a guy. What's your flavor?"

I burst out laughing. "My flavor? I'm pretty sure it's guys, but I don't need to date. I just want to live my life quietly and peacefully. Just having friends and being in one place is amazing."

She smiled as she sat back down across from me. I took another swallow of my coffee. "This is so tasty. I still can't believe the blackberry works with this."

Casey waggled her brows. "Do you think the donuts are cool enough for us to have one?" she asked, eyeing them.

"Of course." I reached over, spinning the tray around. "Should we sprinkle powdered sugar on them?"

Casey grinned. "Yes, please!"

Whenever I made batches of donuts, there were always a few bits of dough left over, so I made small ones for the staff here. Casey was partial to the cake donuts with powdered sugar. I slipped off my stool and snagged two plates and the small shaker of powdered sugar.

A moment later, Casey took a bite of one, letting out a happy hum. "So good!" she enthused after she finished chewing. "How did you learn to bake so well if you were growing up in an RV? I know there are fancy RVs, but still, it seems like the kitchen situation would be limited."

I laughed softly. "I made do. It was one of the few things that my mom let me do off-camera. My grandma taught me how to bake when I was little. She's the reason I'm back in Willow Brook."

"Is she here?" Casey asked.

"Yup, I live right next door to her. I was born here. My grandma has some health issues, and I'm a little worried about her, so I wanted to be close to her."

"Is she okay?" Casey looked worried.

Every time I considered this, a little spurt of anxiety went through me. "Well, she's in her seventies and—" I took a quick breath, taking a bite of my donut and chewing my anxiety away. "She let me move in beside her in a little cabin she used to rent out on her property. Her mind is still ringing on all bells, but her knees hurt all the time, and I worry about her falling."

"Oh, Luna, that's not easy." Casey's warm gaze held me. "Anything you need, I will do it."

"Can you turn back time and make her about twenty years younger?" I teased lightly.

"If I could, I would."

———

A little while later, Casey was busy in the front, Janet was bustling around in the back, and I was boxing up donuts to sell. I swear my body had an antenna for Parker. I'd thought he was cute before, but there were tons of cute guys in the world. He had a different effect on me, and I was still trying to convince myself he wasn't who I thought he might be.

I'd been trying to ignore the sparks that exploded inside my body whenever I heard Parker's voice. Just then, I heard the low rumble of his voice as Casey took his order and joked with him about something. And then, "Luna?" she called.

"Yeah?" I hurried toward the waist-high door from the kitchen and looked over it. As soon as my eyes landed on Parker, those sparks scattered through me again.

"Parker needs two boxes of donuts. Do you have that many left?" Casey asked.

I cleared my throat. "Um, yeah. Any requests?"

"Two variety boxes would be great." Parker's eyes met mine, and I willed the heat blasting through me to cool.

I swallowed. "Just give me a minute."

"Breathe," I whispered to myself. "Breathe."

By the time I got back to the front with the donuts, Casey was busy taking orders from a family. She glanced over quickly. "He's already paid."

I rounded the counter to where Parker was waiting. "Here you go," I squeaked.

His eyes met mine. "I just realized how I know you," he said after a long pause.

I almost blurted out, "Took you long enough," but I managed to keep *that* thought inside.

"Why didn't you say anything?" he asked.

I cleared my throat. "I don't know. At first, I wasn't sure, and then I guess I figured you forgot." My cheeks were on freaking fire.

"Before yesterday, I thought I knew you, but I couldn't place you."

"Uh-huh." I cleared my throat. "It's been, you know, over a decade." My breath kept catching as nervousness spun like a storm inside.

Parker's espresso eyes searched mine. "You just disappeared," he finally said.

Because that's what I did. Not like I'd had a choice.

"Is your name Luna or Jane?" he asked.

Chapter Six

PARKER

Is your name Luna or Jane?

As she stared up at me blankly, I wondered how many things I didn't know about her, starting with her name.

"Luna," she said, her tone forceful. She gave her head a little shake. "I know the whole thing is strange. I promise I can explain." She looked so earnest and worried, my heart twisted a little.

I *really* wanted that explanation. "I'd say let's get coffee, but you work here."

Luna's curls bounced as she nodded. "I don't know, um, we could get pizza or something. I really *do* want to explain," she said hurriedly. "I know I should've said something before, but—" Her breath came out in a rushed sigh. "I was embarrassed because you didn't remember me."

"Well, I thought your name was Jane," I pointed out. "You look familiar, but it's been ten years. Your hair was straight back then, and you said your name was Jane." I lifted my hands and let them fall, unsure of what else to say. I experienced a twinge of guilt that I somehow didn't completely recognize her, but people look similar in the world, and I'd chalked it up to that.

"Well, I have your number, Fuzzy loves you, and you've offered to be my dog sitter." I sucked in a breath, trying to collect myself. "Were you ever going to tell me?"

Luna nodded. "I promise I was. I was just trying to figure out when. Until yesterday morning, I only saw you here every so often, and that time you scooped me out of the ocean. I wanted to say something then, but it was a weird day. I was a little flustered yesterday morning because well, the moose and falling in the mud and—" She circled her hand in the air nervously.

"I get it," I finally said after a pocket of silence stretched between us. "For what it's worth, I understand keeping things private." When I'd met Luna before, it was a time filled with secrets for me. She sure as hell didn't know my whole story.

She twisted her hands nervously. "I have to get in the back because I'm in the middle of baking."

"I'll text you," I said. "I can grab dinner any night I'm in town."

Her lips curled in a slight smile. "That would be great."

"Your donuts are the best I've ever had, by the way." I lifted the boxes in my hands in emphasis.

My heart felt pulled toward her when her cheeks went pretty and pink again. "I'm glad."

She spun around and hurried into the back. I watched her go and remembered the Luna I'd met for a very brief time years back, a mere two weeks after I got out of juvenile detention.

Chapter Seven

PARKER

Approximately 10 years ago

The cool air feels amazing on my cheeks. I stand on the docks in Fireweed Harbor and take a slow breath.

A few minutes later, I walk along the beach, idly kicking a rock. These days, my social life is pretty empty. In two days, I'm moving to Juneau. I'm going to miss my dad, but my dad is a big part of the reason I don't have many friends because, well, that's a long story.

Fresh out of juvenile detention, all I want is a chance to stay out of trouble. My probation officer has set me up with a job training program in Juneau. I'll be volunteering at the local fire station and training to be a firefighter.

At the sound of footsteps behind me, I glance

back to see a girl. Her dark hair is long and straight. It blows like a banner in the wind behind her. She laughs when a seal pokes its head out of the water and dives back under.

"You can't catch me!" she calls.

I can't stop the laugh that sputters out. She glances over to see me and stops in the sand before slapping her hand over her mouth.

"Don't worry about me. Keep playing hide and seek with the seal," I tease.

I'm drawn to her. Without thinking, I walk across the sand and pebble beach to stop a few feet away from her. "I'm Parker," I say.

She blinks before her lips curl in a slow smile. "I'm—" There's a long enough hesitation that I start to wonder. "Jane," she says, almost a little too forcefully.

"Nice to meet you, Jane." I hold my hand out.

She looks delighted as she smiles down at my hand, reaching out to clasp it and shake it slowly. "Nice to meet you, Parker."

She's so fresh and cute, I want to kiss her. I try to remember the last time I kissed a girl. I have to think a little harder than I would like. It was before detention when I had a girlfriend in high school named Sandra. We officially broke up when I got in trouble, for good reason.

Reluctantly, I release Jane's hand and stuff both

of mine in my pockets as I tip my head to the side. "Are you from here?"

Jane shakes her head, her hair swinging a little. "Just visiting."

She doesn't explain further. I don't know why, but it feels like there's more to it than that. I tell myself I'm a little crazy. Alaska is tourists galore in the summer, so it's perfectly logical for someone to be visiting.

"What are you doing this afternoon?" I ask.

Jane's smile is a little shy. "I'm walking on the beach. I have three hours of freedom. What are you doing?"

"I'm walking on the beach too."

We stare at each other long enough it starts to feel awkward. I'm relieved when she asks, "Can we walk together?"

There's something almost pure about Jane. As if though the very idea of walking with someone on the beach is a novelty. In my case, it is. Ever since I got out of detention, I've been walking on the beach every chance I get, but it's always alone. It's just nice to walk. There's something that feels so free about it.

I hope I never lose my appreciation of the small things. I didn't realize how much I didn't appreciate them until I had to spend time in detention all because I was a dumbass. Fortunately, Jane knows nothing about me. Otherwise, she might not want to walk with me.

We fall into step beside each other. It's quiet at first. After a while, Jane nudges me with her elbow. "Tell me something about yourself."

"What do you mean?"

"Well, are you from here?" she presses.

I smile down at her. "Mostly. I grew up in Alaska. I've lived with my dad here, in Skagway, Juneau, and even up in Fairbanks."

"Just you and your dad?"

Pain strums an old chord in my heart. "Yup. My mom is long gone," I say. "It's just me and my dad." I clear my throat. "Where are you from?"

"Alaska," she says simply.

A chuckle rustles in my throat. To some, that answer might not make sense, but if you're from Alaska, it does. Alaska's freaking huge, geographically speaking, but it's small as far as the feeling of being from here. It's wildness bonds you to each other.

"Anywhere specific in Alaska, or just the whole state?" I tease lightly.

She grins up at me. "I was born in Willow Brook, but I've lived all over. My parents have an RV, so we're driving around Alaska this summer."

Yet again, I have a feeling there are some big gaps in that description. There's a powerful sense of loneliness emanating from her, and I don't like it.

She shouldn't feel lonely, but then I know the feeling well.

"Well, that's cool," I say, keeping my tone casual. I can't even wrap my brain around how I feel with her. There's a sense of comfort I've never experienced this quickly. With anyone.

We walk for close to three hours. I take her along a trail nearby that leads to a waterfall that I used to go to when I was a little kid.

Just when I've lost track of time, she announces, "I have to go back."

I don't want her to go back, yet I know that's not rational. I look down at her, lost in the moment that stretches between us, shimmering and alive. Her blue eyes are layered in color. Looking into them is like staring into the ocean when the sun filters through it. I don't realize I've taken a step closer and reached for her hand until I feel her fingers lace with mine. A pink flush rises on her cheeks, and I notice the spray of freckles across her nose.

"I like you, Parker," Jane says, her words coming out in a rush.

I take an unsteady breath. "I like you." My voice almost sounds a little rusty, and I have to clear my throat.

She blinks up at me and takes another step, placing her palm on my chest. My heart kicks toward her touch.

"What if I want to see you again?" I hear myself asking.

I could swear there's a sheen of tears in Jane's eyes. "I wish," she whispers. "But I don't live here."

I want to ask her for her phone number, but I don't even have my own phone. As if she's reading my mind, she says, "And I don't have a phone. If I did, I'd give you my number."

"It's okay. I don't have a phone either."

I'm trying to tell myself I shouldn't kiss her, but she startles me by leaning up and pressing her lips to mine. She jumps back quickly. "I probably shouldn't have done that!"

"Don't say that," I tell her.

"If I'm never going to see you again, a kiss is a good memory," she says softly.

"We could try again," I say, my heart pounding so hard it hurts.

Jane blinks up at me before nodding. Time feels as if it's moving in slow motion as I take a tiny step closer to her. Her palm is still resting over my heart, and she slides an arm around my waist as I do the same. I hold her gaze as I lower my head. I hear the echoing drumroll of my heartbeat, the rush of blood in my ears, and the distant screech of an eagle, followed by the chatter of a magpie.

There's a splash in the water just as I bring my lips to Jane's. She holds completely still for a moment before she lets out a soft sigh into our kiss. I can't help myself and take the kiss deeper. I slide my tongue across the seam of her lips. She opens easily, her tongue gliding against mine.

I'm tumbling into this moment with her. My knees are almost wobbly by the time we break apart, both of us nearly desperate for air. Jane takes a shaky breath as my heart pounds against her palm.

"That was my first kiss," she says. "Thank you for making it amazing."

I feel small in this moment, as if I can't quite rise to it. The way it feels to stand here holding her, the way it feels to kiss her is all more than I ever could've imagined. Jane feels good and pure. If she knew my story, she probably never would've spent these hours walking on the beach with me. These hours will be a memory I tuck into my pocket and pull out on a bad day.

"You're the first girl I've ever felt like this with," I surprise myself by saying.

"I will not forget you, Parker. Maybe someday I'll see you again."

I walk with her back to the harbor. The last I see of her is when she presses her fingers to her lips and blows me a kiss.

Chapter Eight

LUNA

Even though I've seen Parker a few times in the café, and he rescued me in the ocean, a corner of my mind never stopped questioning if it was really him. This version of Parker was taller and more built than the Parker I'd spent a few halcyon hours with a decade ago.

I'd never seen him after that. I'd wanted to stay in Fireweed Harbor because it was a cute little town, but my parents had insisted on sticking to their plan to create content. We'd left the following morning.

When Parker had scooped me out of the ocean that day a few months ago, I'd been so befuddled, I couldn't think too clearly, and doubts still crowded my mind. It wasn't until this morning after the moose incident that I felt that same feeling with him. I felt *safe* with him. And now, I had to explain why I gave him a fake name before. Even though my parents had screwed up a lot of stuff when they were dragging me along in their influencer life, they'd insisted on giving me a different public name. My mom had also straightened my unruly curls religiously.

Between my name and my straight hair, my parents hoped to protect me somehow. I guess they did a little. No one had ever recognized me since I'd left that life. All this to say, I'd never gotten close enough to someone in real life for them to connect the dots.

My parents' travel channel was successful enough for them to make a living, but never successful enough for them to stop. They made enough from ads to pay for gas money and whatever other bills we had. Their high hopes had only taken them so far.

With a quiet sigh, I continued boxing up donuts, mulling over how to handle this situation with Parker. Part of me thrilled to the idea that we somehow ended up in the same place. I'd never forgotten that kiss.

I'd only told one person about it, who'd promptly told my parents. Then, my parents wanted to do a whole episode on it. I had to beg them to the point of tears to talk them out of it. It was one of the few times they'd actually respected my wishes. Other private conversations I'd been forced to have on camera included my mom buying a box of tampons for me when I got my period, my mom helping me pick out a bra, and me struggling through math homework.

Surprisingly, they hadn't filmed when I was practicing baking. They always wanted to put the uncomfortable awkward moments on camera. Those got more views and, in turn, more money. The travel itself became exhausting. While Alaska was big geographically, there were only so many chances for social interactions. Most years, we traveled to the lower 48 for the winter.

I didn't think I ever wanted to travel again in my life. I took an unsteady breath and shook my thoughts away. As I finished boxing up the last box of donuts, Casey popped into the back. "I just sold all of those!"

I looked at the stack of ten boxes, my mouth dropping open as I turned back toward her. "All of them?" I squeaked.

"Luna, your donuts are famous." Casey bounced on her toes. "Seriously."

"Um, I don't think my donuts are famous."

"They're famous here, and that's all that matters." She began stacking the boxes. When her gaze swung to mine again, she stopped. "Are you okay?"

I meant to keep it all together, but the next thing I knew, tears were splashing onto my cheeks. I didn't know what to say. Just then, Josie came walking in from the break room. I hadn't even realized she was back there. "What's happening?" she asked.

The second she saw my face, and before I could even say a word, Josie raced across the kitchen and pulled me into a big hug. Like Casey, Josie gave good hugs. Actually, every friend I met in Willow Brook gave the best hugs.

"What's wrong?" she demanded when she stepped back.

I swiped at my tears with my fingertips and sniffled. "It's way too much to explain right now."

Janet's voice came from the front, calling for Casey. "I need to—" I didn't know what I needed, but it was too busy here for me to fall apart.

Josie nodded. "You hold that thought. We have card night coming up, and you're gonna fill us all in on what's going on."

I took a shaky breath as I nodded. As recently as a day ago, I wouldn't have wanted to tell an entire group of people my whole story, yet it suddenly felt like a huge relief. I needed some advice. I also desperately wanted to stop feeling like I had to keep my past a secret. On top of that, I definitely needed help to figure out how to explain the mess to Parker.

"Okay," I said firmly.

Josie thrust a box of tissues in my hand. I blew my nose and dabbed at my eyes as Casey hurried to the front while Janet came bustling in the back.

"Luna, can you stay and make some more

donuts?” Janet asked as she made a beeline for the dishwasher with a tray full of dirty dishes in hand. “Pretty please. We’re completely out in the front.” She glanced over her shoulder, caught a look at me, and skidded to a stop. “Are you okay, hon?”

“Yes,” I replied, even though it had to be obvious I’d just been crying. “I really am,” I insisted when Janet tipped her head to the side, her brow crinkling with worry.

“Luna is okay,” Josie said. “Well, maybe not right this second, but she will be.”

A laugh sputtered up. Janet quickly put down the dish tray before walking over to give me a big hug. “You will be okay,” she announced.

“I know.” And, I did know. The reservoir of strength from my friends buoyed me. I didn’t think I’d ever get enough of all the hugs around here.

Janet smiled softly. “Good. Can you stay and make more donuts?” she repeated.

“Absolutely.”

Josie squeezed my shoulder as she wrapped an apron around her waist. “You bake. I gotta get out front. It sounds nuts out there.”

“One of those tour buses is here,” Janet tossed over her shoulder as she hurried out of the kitchen.

I settled into making another batch of dough for donuts. I loved it here. My grandmother had suggested asking Janet about baking here. My original plan had been to just use the kitchen, but then Janet wanted to sell the donuts. I was making enough from the donuts that it would keep me afloat financially while I tried to figure out my next steps.

Janet returned to the kitchen and began prepping the other items she baked for the café. With Janet and my grandmother old friends, she knew my story and me pretty well.

She glanced up at one point as we worked. "I hope you'll be more open with your friends."

When I lifted my focus to her, the warmth in her gaze made my heart squeeze. "I'm trying," I said.

Her smile was soft. "I know you are. I'm really glad you're here."

"I am too." I swallowed through the emotion tightening in my throat. It meant so much to have a place to stay, to feel like I could belong somewhere instead of feeling adrift in a traveling life.

"I have an idea," she said a moment later.

"Well, I love hearing your ideas, Janet," I said lightly.

"What if you took over all of the baking here?"

My gaze whipped up to hers. My surprise must've shown because she chuckled. "I'm not that young, and I love it here, but I need a plan."

"What do you mean?" Worry spun through me.

"Oh, I'm healthy, Luna, don't you worry about that. But I'm not getting any younger, and I'm close to seven decades. It's coming faster than I would like. I hope to live for a whole century, which wouldn't be crazy because my mom got close to that. But—" She took a quick breath. "I don't have any children. I think of many people in town as my honorary children, but you have a special place in my heart. What if I stay on and "manage"—" She used air quotes for that. "And eventually you take over the whole thing. I promise you it's profitable."

Flummoxed, I stared at her, my mouth dropping open. For entirely different reasons than earlier, tears stung my eyes again. "What are you even talking about?"

"I'm talking about giving you this café," she said firmly. "Not right away. You do your donuts and take over the baking, but in the long run, I would give this place to you. We're talking some years down the road. As long as I stay healthy, I still want to work. But I'm not territorial. You can change it to fit with your donuts. I think those alone could be a whole business. Jasmine rents the space in the back for her pottery studio, but there's room in the garage behind us that you could update for a bigger baking kitchen if you ever wanted."

"I didn't even know that was part of this," I said slowly, envisioning the square steel garage back there.

Janet nodded. "I own it. It came with the property. They used to use it for storage for the fire station, and I would rent it to them, but they don't need it anymore ever since they expanded the new station. I was thinking, while I'm still in charge here, you could get that up and running for your bakery."

I couldn't really absorb all of this. "Um, I could pay rent," I said.

"Luna, I don't need the rent. I own all of this free and clear. This café is really profitable, in part because I don't have to worry about overhead except for paying staff and utilities. That's why I pay everybody well. Restaurants either fail or they do amazing. I've lucked out here, maybe because I kept it simple. That's my best advice to you. If you want this place, when you're ready, just keep it simple."

Overcome with emotion, all I could do was gape at her. I'd known Janet my whole life, but I didn't get to see her much because we didn't come back often after my parents started traveling. Whenever we came back to visit, I was pretty sure my mom got an earful from my grandma, so they only came on the holidays.

I was silent long enough that Janet's brow furrowed. "Luna, you don't have to do this. I just—"

"Oh, I definitely want to do this, but I don't want to take anything from you. At all."

Janet smiled softly. "I love it here. This place is part of me, but I've thought long and hard about this. I've known for a while that I need some kind of plan. When you finally came home, I knew you were the plan. Your grandma is one of my best friends, and I love her to pieces. She has worried and worried and worried about you. When I told her I've been thinking about this, she thought it might be a great idea. She told me you don't want to leave Willow Brook again."

I shook my head emphatically. "Definitely not." I paused, an old pain stinging in my heart. "I don't want to travel. I've done enough of that. More than anything in the world, I want to be in one place. Willow Brook is where I was born and where I always wanted to come back to. I guess because when I was here, I felt—" I considered my words. "Settled. Maybe because of Gram being here."

"Well, here's the status. I've already talked to my attorney about it. Not just for you, but whatever I do, I need to know how to handle it. We could meet with her together, and she'll line out how we need to handle it. For now, as far as baking full-time, your donuts are your thing. I don't want to change that. For the other baking, how about I pay you an hourly wage? I can also add you to our health insurance. You need to work here twenty-five hours per week to qualify for that."

"I am one hundred percent on board with this plan!"

Janet knew about my heart issue and that health insurance was a big deal for me. At the moment, I was paying through the nose for it.

She beamed. "Perfect! How about you start baking next week?"

"Works for me. Do I need to figure out a schedule with you?"

She shrugged. "Let me know what works for you. As long as we have the baked goods, I don't care when you do the work."

"I love you, Janet! I'd hug you, but I can't." I held up my hands, which were currently dusted in flour. "Air hugs."

As the day went on, Josie and Casey heard the news about me coming on to bake full-time, and they were both ecstatic. Janet and I decided to wait on discussing any plans for me to take over the cafe until we hammered the details out and actually confirmed it.

That afternoon, as I was leaving, my phone vibrated. I glanced down to see a text from Parker. *Pizza?*

Chapter Nine

PARKER

"Parker!" my dad's voice boomed through the phone.

"Hey, Dad," I replied with a low chuckle.

"Just calling to see how you're doing."

"I'm doing," I replied. "How are you and Elaine doing?"

"Good, good. I was actually calling to tell you we eloped," he said as calmly as if he were sharing about the weather that day.

"Seriously?" I sputtered.

"Completely. I just needed to grow up and discover Elaine was special." My dad sounded downright giddy about this news, his voice jovial.

"Oh, wow. Have you told Stella yet?" I asked, referring to my sister.

"Just got off the phone with her. We're planning a poor man's cruise for our honeymoon on the ferry.

We got our own cabin and everything. There's a stop in the Anchorage port, so we're hoping to see you and Stella. We can rent a car and drive to Willow Brook."

"Well, congrats. Text me the details for when you plan to visit. Of course, I'll plan on meeting you one way or another when you're nearby."

"Awesome!"

My dad and I chatted for a few more minutes before he asked, "You seeing anyone? I kind of think it's your turn."

My mind instantly flashed to Luna, dialing back to the memory of that single kiss with her that afternoon years ago. Those few hours with her burned so deeply in my memory, every encounter with anyone since then had fallen short. And yet, I didn't even know who she was. Not really.

"Parker?" my dad prompted.

I kicked my thoughts on track. "Not seeing anyone at the moment, Dad. I know you have high hopes," I teased lightly.

"I just—" His voice hitched. "I love you, son. And, I know I kind of screwed up your childhood, but I want the best for you."

"Dad," I cut in. "Maybe things weren't perfect when I was growing up, but I'm pretty sure nobody's childhood is perfect. I always knew you loved me, and that's the most important part. I'm just really glad you feel good about your life now. My life's pretty good too. I have a job I love, I live somewhere beautiful, and I have good friends. I have you, and now, I guess a stepmom. It's all good."

A few beats of quiet echoed through the call. "I'm glad for all that, but I hate that you ended up in detention because I was a dumbass."

I bit back a sigh. "Dad, things go the way they go. If there's one thing we can't change, it's the past. I figure I learned a lot from that, so stop worrying about it. Okay? I don't worry about it. I met Hudson there, and he's my best friend."

"All right, all right. I'll try not to worry," my dad muttered.

"Don't they tell you in your groups to let go, let God, and all that. You made your amends with me. Honestly, maybe you didn't always make the best decisions, but I never doubted you were there for me, and not everyone gets that in life."

Another sigh filtered through the call. He was big on the sighs when he was worried. "I love you, Parker. I'll text you the dates for when we set up our trip."

"Looking forward to seeing you. Love you too."

When I tapped to end the call, I stared at the picture of my dad saved with his contact in my phone. His hair was mussed, and he wore a goofy grin. I still marveled that he and my half-sister's mom had reconnected. The modern miracle of DNA testing had brought them together. My sister

Stella's mom hadn't been busy running drugs like my dad, but from what I understood, she hadn't had the most stable life.

That's how my dad got me in trouble. He thought it would be great for me to help him sell drugs in high school. I shook my head, almost bemused now. Every word I told him was true. I was over it. It was a lesson I had to learn. Maybe he'd been the one to lead me to that path, but, at the time, it held powerful temptations for me. Money, street cred, and a few other dumb things had seemed important when I was young and stupid.

To this day, I never forgot something the public defender assigned to me had said. I'd written it down and covered it with clear tape. I still kept it in my wallet. Pulling it out, I read it once again. *Don't judge yourself for your worst days. There's more to you than that.*

I had met Hudson in detention and would always consider him one of my best friends. We hadn't stayed in touch for a chunk of time because that was before cell phones were ubiquitous. Needless to say, both of us had been poor and broke with dads who weren't financially stable. We hadn't been able to stay in touch, but I was beyond grateful life had brought us back together. We'd both ended up doing firefighter training and becoming hotshots. We'd even managed to get through him falling in love with my half-sister.

I'd been a little overprotective at first, but Stella had put me in my place on that. With a mental shake, I snagged my keys and headed out the door.

When I glanced down at my phone screen once I climbed into my truck, I saw Luna had finally replied to my text. *Sure! Tomorrow?*

Even though a tiny part of me thought maybe I should delay it and play it cool, I ended up replying right away.

Me: *Sounds good. Should I pick you up?*

Luna: *That would be great. You know where I live.*

Anticipation hummed through me. I was impatient to see her again. More than that, I was impatient to understand why she used a fake name before. In reality, I recognized that when we spent that hazy, dreamy afternoon together, I'd been a complete stranger to her. Maybe it had been safest for her to call herself Jane instead of giving me her real name. I still wanted to understand why.

———

Hudson leaned back in his chair, chuckling at a comment Griffin had made. "Dude, you have to decide. It's a choice between fewer fish and a pretty boat ride."

"Or more fish and bigger fish," Leo added.

"I prefer the Kenai River. China Poot's beautiful,

but it's really only worth it if you live nearby," I pointed out.

"What's the difference?" Kincaid asked.

Kincaid was not only new to our crew, but he was new to Alaska. He seemed like a solid guy. Cade, a superintendent on a different crew, leaned forward. "Okay, here's the deal. For dipnetting in this area, the main choices are Kenai River, Kasilof River, or China Poot Bay, which is across Kachemak Bay. You can only get one permit every year. China Poot is six fish for every trip. Kenai and Kasilof are twenty-five fish overall. For families, it's another ten fish for every other person in the family. Personally, I prefer the Kenai River. The fish are bigger, so you get the most for the work. Kasilof River is nice, but the fish are smaller. Some people like China Poot, but you have to make four trips to get the same number of fish. Although it's totally beautiful and the fish literally swim over a waterfall. Once was enough for me. I go to the Kenai River," Cade said with a tap of his fingers on the table.

"Wow," Kincaid replied. "Sign me up." He chuckled.

"How long you been in Alaska?" Graham asked.

"Three months," Kincaid said.

"You'll be able to go next year," Graham said. "You gotta be a resident for a full year before you can get a dipnetting permit. They're strict about that." Graham was the superintendent for our crew and a solid guy.

"I don't mind the wait." Kincaid shrugged.

We were at Wildlands Lodge, a local hotel, bar, and restaurant. It was situated on a lake in the center of town. Even though it was autumn and the height of tourist season was over, the place was packed. It always was. We often got together here for dinner and drinks with anyone who wanted to tag along from the fire station. Willow Brook was a hub for four hotshot crews, along with a local crew, which meant for a lot of firefighters in town. Lately, we stayed busy with fires popping up all the time, with summers getting longer and hotter on the West Coast, and Alaska a busy place for wildfires. I loved my job, and I loved the wilderness.

Conversation carried on as everybody shared their opinions on dipnetting and debated favorite local fishing places.

I glanced toward Hudson. "Did Stella tell you about the elopement? Is that what we call it?"

Hudson flashed a smile. "Guess so, and yeah, she did."

"Good for them." I chuckled. "My dad is one happy guy. He said they're doing a ferry trip for their honeymoon. He said they want to try to meet up with us when they stop in Anchorage."

"We'll plan on it. Let's just hope we're not out at a fire," Hudson said.

"Let's hope," I replied.

Hudson waggled his brows. "Stella tells me your dad is worried about making sure you fall in love."

I shook my head slowly as I pressed my tongue into my cheek. "I know. Let's get real. When my dad was my age, he wasn't serious with anyone, like ever. He was busy selling drugs. No judgment. He had his shit to figure out, and he's doing well now. I love him, but I think it's fucking hysterical. He thinks it's time for me to fall in love and settle down. Of course, you and Stella just did, so there's that." I ran a hand through my hair with a sigh.

Hudson clapped me on the shoulder. "I think it's funny. Your dad's a lot like mine. I love my dad, and he cracks me up. He's happy as can be these days with his girlfriend." Hudson's gaze sobered. He rested an elbow on the table and took a swallow of beer. "I'm the first to say I never thought falling in love would matter, but it's the best thing that ever happened to me."

I pondered his observation as I drove home later. Fuzzy would be waiting at home, always happy to see me. And yet, I lived a pretty solitary life. I was also acutely aware of just how impatient I was to see Luna again.

Chapter Ten

LUNA

"Your parents are the Talton's who have that RV channel?" Maisie stared at me, her eyes wide.

I nodded. "They sure are. I went by Jane on the channel. They didn't want me to use my real first name, and they straightened my hair."

She pointed at her own curls and shook her head. "That must've been a chore."

"It was," I replied dryly.

Stella, who was sitting beside Maisie at the table, slid her gaze to the side. "Are you really into following RV influencers online?"

Maisie shrugged. "I wouldn't say I follow them, but I watch sometimes. There's no way I would live a life like that with my kids, but it seems, I don't know, carefree."

Madison, who was seated across from Maisie, cleared her throat. "It's your turn."

Maisie quickly refocused her attention on her cards. Casey had brought me along for card night with this group of women. I'd known many of them when I was a little girl, but since we'd started traveling when I was still in elementary school, it felt like I was getting to know them all over again. Most of us didn't actually play cards, but there were a few who took it seriously, including Maisie, who usually won.

Tonight, we were at Tish and Griffin's house with Griffin out with his friends. We were taking turns cooing over Tish's little boy, Teddy, a cute little toddler.

He was sound asleep in Tiffany's lap at the moment. She glanced over to Tish. "Should we just put him to bed?" she whispered.

Tish nodded and scooped him out of Tiffany's arms. Teddy didn't even open his eyes as Tish carried him away.

"Babies are so cute," Tiffany said when she glanced to me.

"Babies are cute," I agreed. "Is he still a baby? At what age do babies become toddlers? I don't actually know this."

Maisie snorted when she looked up from her cards. "I don't know what the rules are, but I say after they turn one. They're heavy then," she pointed out.

"Speaking of age," Casey chimed in. "How old were you when your parents started doing this RV influencer life? I zigzagged all the way from the coast of North Carolina to Alaska. It was fun and nice to see the views, and I don't regret doing it, but that's a lot of driving. I can't imagine doing that and not having an end date to a trip like that."

Maisie played another card, nodding as she glanced up. "Yeah, I don't even know how parents can handle that, to be honest. It would be much harder to create structure for kids."

"I ended up hating it," I said, that familiar bitterness lacing my words.

Tiffany's eyes went wide. "You sound like you really hated it."

A sigh slipped out. "At first, when my parents told me that was their plan, I thought it would be cool. It was fun for maybe six months. There are cool places that I got to visit. I've been to every state, and I've seen most of the main parks and places like the Grand Canyon, the Badlands, the Catskills and Adirondacks, the Blue Ridge Mountains, coastal Maine, and more. All of it beautiful. They didn't tell me at the beginning about their plan to create content." I rolled my eyes. "I'm the first to say there's a lot of cool stuff that can happen online.

That's where I go when I need to learn something. That's how I learned to make donuts. My grandmother used to bake with me when we visited here in Willow Brook and then I would practice by myself. But I got sick of my life being online. I got so tired of having my hair straightened. I got tired of being called Jane. It was just me and my parents all the time. My mom signed me up for online school and I didn't really have any friends. I had one person who I thought was my friend, and—" I paused as my heart twisted in my chest. "Her parents were also RV influencers. I didn't know they got a cut from my parents' ad money every time we did stuff together. Since my parents were more successful, they made sure Margie hung out with me."

Tiffany curled her arm around my shoulders and squeezed. "Luna! I don't like that," she said with feeling.

I returned her side hug. "I didn't like it either. It hurt. And the stuff you see online are the clips that they make perfect. I got so tired of everything being recorded. I never even had a boyfriend." My cheeks puffed when I let out a big sigh. "I love my parents even though I didn't like that. They're still doing it and they're pretty upset I'm not there anymore. I think they had this idea, I'm not freaking kidding, that I would stay with them after I became an adult. I think they hoped they'd end up with grandkids on the channel. Although I have no idea how they thought I'd manage to meet someone and have anything resembling a relationship." I shook my head. "There need to be laws that protect kids from this shit."

Maisie caught my eye. "Hearing this is so sad. I do watch these short clips, but I don't want to anymore. I'm so sorry you went through that."

"When people ask me about the channel, I usually say they should stick to watching creators who don't do the family stuff. That way, you don't have to wonder how the kids are affected," I said.

"Are you glad they had you go by Jane?" Casey asked.

I nodded. "That was one thing my parents did right. Although I was annoyed with it at the time, now I'm really glad I'm just Luna. I've never been recognized in the wild, or at least not by anyone who told me. Not since I stopped straightening my hair and started using my real name, which I did the second I moved away."

"How old were you when you stopped?" Phoebe asked.

"I moved out of the RV the day after my eighteenth birthday. I had already talked to my grandmother and she'd opened a bank account for me and sent me enough money to find an apartment and get on my feet. It was spring, so we had just gotten back to Alaska."

"Did you tell your parents you were leaving?" Tiffany asked.

I shook my head. "I called them after I landed in Juneau. They wouldn't have done anything crazy; they're not like that, but they definitely would've tried to talk me out of it. It would've been a big argument with my grandmother. We did Christmas with her every year, mostly because I begged."

"Wow," Madison breathed.

"I don't mean to be that negative about my parents. I love them. They decided they wanted to try it. Once they started making enough money to fund their travel, they just kept doing it, but it ends up—" I paused. "It ends up feeling like you're not doing it for the experience. You're doing it for the content." I looked around the small table at the room of women. "I'm embarrassed to say this, but you all are my first actual friends since I was in elementary school."

Tiffany squeezed me again. "We are absolutely your friends, and we are here for you."

My eyes stung with tears as I took an unsteady breath. "Thank you. I really mean that."

Amelia, who was tall and kind of intimidated me because she ran a construction business and was a badass, caught my eye and smiled. "We really mean it too."

"Thank you," I whispered.

I started to feel a little uncomfortable with all the attention, and because they were my friends, even if these were new friendships for me, they didn't dwell on it. Conversation moved onto lighter topics.

"You'd better be careful if you have a thing against firefighters," Maisie offered wryly after the card game was over a little while later, and we were relaxing around the table, eating off of the dessert tray I'd brought.

"What do you mean?" I asked.

She rolled her eyes. "I cannot believe I'm gonna say this, but falling in love with a firefighter is practically a rite of passage in this town."

I snorted. "I have noticed that," I commented. My gaze arced around the table. "I'm not planning on falling in love with anyone because I'm just figuring out how to be friends and have a normal life."

Casey nudged me with her elbow. "Parker is cute."

"And, he's single," Maisie supplied helpfully.

My cheeks started to burn. Since Maisie was the lead dispatcher at Willow Brook Fire & Rescue, she knew pretty much everything about all the firefighters. Of course, she was also always up to speed on any emergency in town and everyone involved. She was a great source of information.

"Hmm," I replied vaguely.

"Parker's a hot one," Tiffany said. "He's also got that whole mysterious broody thing going on." She waggled her brows.

Amelia cast Tiffany a sly smile. "Wes could be called mysterious and broody," she teased lightly. Wes, being Tiffany's husband and a firefighter.

Tiffany bit her lip as she laughed. "Okay, maybe he could be. He kind of keeps to himself."

Warm-hearted teasing carried on while I savored being with women who weren't spending time with me because I was on my parents' online channel. It was a blessing I'd never take for granted.

Later that night, after I got home, I eyed the text from Parker. My belly felt a little tingly just thinking about him.

I still remembered my first and only kiss. With him. I was embarrassed to even tell him I hadn't kissed anyone since him. Those few hours at the beach with Parker that afternoon felt like a slice of time I snatched out of the universe and kept for myself.

It was rare for my parents to let me wander anywhere when we were traveling. Alaska was the only place where they felt comfortable letting me do my own thing. In hindsight, that was kind of funny because there were moose everywhere, the occasional bear encounter, and plenty of other wildlife to worry about. That afternoon, they were busy because they were updating the registration on the RV and taking care of other things. There was no content to make for that.

———

The following night, Parker looked at me from across the table, and I could've sworn he could read into my muddled, confused heart. I twisted the napkin in my fingers, trying to think of where to start.

Blessedly, the waiter stopped by our table. "It'll be about fifteen minutes for your pizza. We're slammed," he explained, gesturing around the packed dining area. "Can I get you anything to drink other than water?"

Parker tilted his head as he glanced back over at me with an arched brow. "Just water." I cleared my throat because my voice sounded squeaky.

"That's it for me as well," Parker replied.

After the waiter had walked away, Parker added, "Dinner is on me. I invited you."

"I know, but—" I twisted the napkin as I tried to gather some courage.

"What's wrong?" he asked, his gaze concerned.

Before I could think it through, my words tumbled out. "I'm afraid that you're gonna be mad at me for telling you my name was Jane, but that was the name I went by back when we met because my parents were, well, they *are* RV influencers. They have a whole channel online, and that was my life then."

His eyes went wide. "What? RV what?"

Although this wasn't how I had planned to explain everything, I was relieved to talk about it. "So when I was about—" I paused, mentally counting. "Eight years old. My parents decided they wanted to take off in an RV. My dad had started repairing one and was posting about it online. You know how people do that. Anyway, so they wanted to make enough money with ads to live off it, so they started a whole channel and that became my life. They didn't protect me from much, but they decided to have me go by Jane online and they straightened my hair. When you met me then, that's why my hair was straight and why I said my name was Jane."

Parker stared at me so long, I shifted restlessly in my seat. "Uh, wow," he finally said slowly. "I know that's a thing, but are you for real?"

I was mortified, just miserable, inside. "Oh, it's a thing. There are lots of families who do it. Do you watch any of those online short video channels?"

He shook his head slowly. "It's not like I don't see stuff online, but it's not a big part of my life. I have email, but I'm not on social media at all. At the time you met me, I didn't even have a cell phone because—" He took a deep breath. "You go ahead, and I'll explain my life afterwards."

"There's not much else to explain. Do you hate

me for lying?" Anxiety swirled inside, a restless storm in my chest.

"Luna, no! I knew I sort of recognized you and something felt familiar, but I couldn't figure it out. I never forgot you. I guess I'm relieved now that I understand why you went by a different name and why your hair was straight." He smiled slowly. "Your curls are pretty."

Heat flared in my cheeks as I held his gaze. "Well, that's good because I'm never straightening my hair again."

Parker threw his head back with a laugh. "I love your curls. So what happened after that time we met?"

"I was seventeen and in my last year of high school. As soon as I turned eighteen, I found a job in Juneau. I'm still in touch with my parents, and I love them, but I'm never living that life again. Ever. I was so tired of it. I'm just so relieved you don't hate me."

I hadn't realized how much I'd worried about this until now, when the tension I'd been carrying inside started to ease. "I lied to you that day. I didn't want to tell you the whole thing at the time because I was afraid of what you might think. When I first saw you here, I wasn't sure it was you either. You didn't seem to recognize me and so it seemed best to leave it alone." I took a quick breath, needing the courage from a blast of oxygen. "I wanted you to like me for me."

"I did," he said softly.

That two-word reply sent a jolt of joy through me. We smiled at each other. I felt a little goofy, a sense of giddiness rising inside. "So, um, tell me your story."

Parker's shoulders rose when he took a deep breath. "For what it's worth, you might not wanna talk to me after I tell you my story."

"Parker, I doubt that. You're friends with all my friends here. I know you're a nice guy."

He was quiet as he held my gaze for a long beat. Just then, our waiter arrived to set plates down in front of us. "Five more minutes for the pizza," he announced before hurrying off.

"I didn't have a cell phone when you and I met because I'd just gotten out of juvenile detention," Parker said flatly.

"You mean like jail for teenagers?" I asked.

"Exactly that," he said. "I haven't even gotten a parking ticket since then. I ended up a hotshot fire-fighter because the vocational program my proba-tion officer set me up with included volunteering for community service at a fire station and training to be a hotshot firefighter. I went to detention because I got caught dealing drugs in high school. I have all kinds of reasons for why that happened, including that my dad did it at the time, but in the end, I still have to be accountable. He doesn't do illegal things anymore either. I promise you. Me and Stella share a dad. He's doing good now, he's walking the straight and narrow, but—" He paused, taking a slow breath as he leaned his head back. He leveled his gaze with mine again. "Are you ready to run away now?" He gestured his thumb toward the door.

I rested my elbows on the table and leaned toward him. "Absolutely not. Life happens, Parker. I've heard Stella's story about how she connected with you, but I didn't know all of this. Hudson's pretty open about what happened to him. My grandmother always tells me the mistakes we make are the lessons we need."

Parker stared at me for a long moment before he reached for my hands. The warmth of his grip felt so good I almost sighed over it.

"Thank you," he said, his voice gruff.

"For what?"

"Not judging me for my screw ups. I did some dumb shit when I was younger and I regret it a lot."

That giddy sense of joy kept spinning in my chest as I savored the feel of Parker's hands around mine. "I may not know much, because my life was kind of odd growing up, but I know you're a good man. I can feel it."

When I squeezed his hands, Parker squeezed back. "Look at that. We got the hard stuff out of the way," he said with a chuckle.

On cue, the waiter arrived, delivering our pizza with a flourish. I reluctantly let go of Parker's hands out of necessity. A few minutes later, we had both taken a few bites of pizza, and Parker paused. "I was pretty sure you'd run for the hills once you heard my history."

"I thought you might think I was crazy because I had a made-up name and straight hair when we met."

His smile was slow and made my belly feel tingly.

"I understand," he said as his smile faded. "I imagine that was kind of an unusual life."

I contemplated the years of being on camera, of so many moments that should've been private being recorded and broadcast to complete strangers. The confusion of trying to find connections with strangers online since I didn't have friends. Sometimes, I would read the comments and feel like those were the people who understood me. The sad twist of learning that the only friend I thought I had, Margie, was just there because her parents dragged her along. Even though that detail was a twist of a knife that I never could get out of my heart, I felt sad for her. I figured she was as lonely as me.

"It was—" I paused, considering my words. "Strange."

"Are you close to your parents now?" Parker asked.

I finished another bite of pizza as I considered that question. "I suppose it depends on what you mean by close. We stay in touch and they come here for the holidays. My grandmother refuses to let them record in the house. I don't hate them for what they did, but I don't think they understood what it meant for our relationship. They were trying to make money off of our life, and my life, and I didn't have a say in it. I love them and I always will, but I hope maybe they'll decide to do something different." I shrugged. "But they're kind of trapped in this cycle."

Parker took a swallow of water. "That sucks," he finally said, summing it up perfectly and simply.

My mouth twisted to the side as I nodded. "Honestly, and maybe this sounds crazy, but your dad getting you caught up in selling drugs is at least more honest than what my parents did."

Parker tipped his head to the side, pressing his lips together before letting out a sharp sigh. "I get what you mean. I love my dad and he's got his own baggage. What your parents did feels more exploitative. My dad fucked up, and I fucked up, and we paid the price. But it was an honest fuck up. A stupid one, at that." Parker rolled his eyes.

"Are you and your dad close now?"

His smile was warm with hints of wistfulness in his gaze. "Yeah. He's doing pretty good these days. Maybe five years ago, he finally got sober. Going to

NA groups is practically a religion for him these days. He keeps himself together. He and Stella's mom reconnected. They're totally in love. I'm happy for them. And—" He let out a little sigh. "Even though he got me into a lot of trouble when I was younger, he was scrambling to get by, and he made some bad choices. As a result, I made bad choices. Live and learn."

"What about your mom?" I asked.

Chapter Eleven

PARKER

What about your mom?

This conversation had started to feel like a confessional. But I figured it made sense for us to get the heavy stuff out of the way. Of course, Luna couldn't know she'd just landed on the deepest wound in my heart.

Mentally marshaling myself, I barreled ahead. "My mom left. The whole reason I didn't know I had a sister was because my mom didn't tell my dad she got pregnant and had me. My dad was the classic young and dumb guy. Like with my mom, he and Stella's mom hooked up. Don't think he was too big on birth control. My dad didn't stay anywhere long back then. Stella's mom did the sensible thing and steered clear of him, and I don't blame her. When I was six, my mom decided she was done with the parenting gig and dropped me off with him." I tried to ignore the pain that burned in my heart. I was in kindergarten when that happened, old enough to have a few memories of my mom. The whole thing sucked."

Luna held my gaze from across the table, sadness flickering in her eyes. "I'm so sorry." She reached over, curling her hand over mine and squeezing.

My throat felt tight, and my heart gave an achy beat. "Thank you."

The waiter stopped to check in with us, refilling our water and moving along. I was grateful, mostly because I needed the interruption.

"Are you okay?" Luna asked.

"It's not like this is news to me. Have we covered all the heavy stuff yet?" I needed to make light of this, if only because letting it weigh on me could suffocate me.

Her eyes were warm. "I think we have." She took a bite of pizza, letting out a satisfied sigh after she finished chewing. "I never forgot you. That day, I wanted to tell you my name wasn't Jane. My parents had drilled it into my head that I couldn't do that, so I didn't." She shook her head, her curls swinging.

My heart felt squeezed tight for a moment as I held her gaze. "I'm really glad I saw you again. I feel ridiculous that I didn't connect the dots sooner. I kept looking at you, thinking you looked familiar, but it's been, what?"

"A decade," Luna supplied helpfully.

My lips curled in a smile as I nodded. "It's been a minute. The different name and your curly hair threw me off."

Her smile was slow as she nodded. "So, you're a firefighter now, do you like it?" she asked.

"I really do. It's not a lifelong job, mostly because it's so physically demanding, but I love it for now. You're a baker and make the best donuts I've ever had." I grinned over at her. "How did you get into that?"

Luna's eyes sparkled. "My grandmother taught me to bake, and it was the only thing I had for myself. Oddly, my parents never wanted to make content from me baking. I guess maybe there are too many baking shows online. I would practice little recipes in the tiny oven in the RV. Once I moved out on my own, I took a job at a small bakery in Juneau and learned a lot more. After I moved back here, my grandmother helped. She's good friends with Janet. Janet told me I could use the ovens at the café before they were open, and she'd sell them. That's been working out really well."

We stared at each other, and I felt downright goofy looking back at her. There was a lightness to Luna. As cynical as she sounded when she spoke about her childhood, there was almost a purity to her, and I loved it. Maybe that's what I'd been drawn to that afternoon years ago. No matter what, I knew

I wanted more with her—more time, more anything she'd give me.

"How's Fuzzy?" Her question punctured my train of thought.

I chuckled because I usually did when I thought of my goofy dog. "He's good. He'll be sad when I get home tonight. He's always a good dog, but he's a little passive aggressive when I'm not home."

"When you've gone out of town for work before, who took care of him?"

"Before I moved here, I had a friend from another crew who was always willing to help out. But now, I know he loves you, and you offered so..." I waggled my brows before adding, "If that's a big ask, just say so."

"Not at all. I love dogs, and I already offered."

When I drove her home a little while later, my mind spun. I wanted all kinds of things with her. And yet, I didn't want to push too far and too fast. Falling in love and getting serious with anyone was something I'd never even contemplated. With one exception. Luna. My memories of that afternoon with her shined so bright, a corner of my mind always wondered if I'd ever see her again.

I rolled to a stop in front of her place. The small A-frame home was tucked into the trees. Luna smiled over at me in the truck, the porch light catching on her curls and shimmering. "Do you want to come in? Just for a few minutes," she added hurriedly.

"I'd love that." I didn't want to leave. At all. I wanted time with her to unspool without end.

When I walked inside with her, I glanced around, again taking in the small space. It had an open layout, but felt cozy. When I'd been here the other day, I wasn't focused on looking around. The hardwood floor had colorful rugs scattered over it. The space felt comfortable and whimsical. There was a couch with cushions and a TV on a low table to the side. There was a single door at the back of the kitchen, which I presumed led to a bathroom.

Luna set her purse on a table by the door and turned to face me, suddenly looking uncertain.

"What is it?" I asked.

Her fingers curled on the hem of her lightweight sweater, rubbing along the edge. "I don't know. I just got nervous."

"I can go," I said quickly, even though I really didn't want to leave. More than that, I didn't want her to feel nervous around me.

Her curls swung as she shook her head quickly. "Please don't go."

We had entered through the back into the kitchen, and we were standing beside her kitchen island. She startled me when she reached out, catching my hand with hers.

"The last time I spent a few hours with you, I

kissed you before I had to go," she said, her voice throaty.

Her words were like a gust of air blown into a low-burning fire, the rush of oxygen sending the flames flickering high. Her hand was cold, and I instinctively curled mine around it.

I had to clear my throat to speak, and my voice came out gruff. "You did."

I wanted to kiss her more than I wanted to breathe, but I waited. I needed for this to be something she wanted. She took a step closer. Just like all those years ago, her palm landed in the center of my chest. My pulse lunged and my heart felt physically pulled forward again, as if reaching for the connection.

Her pink flush deepened, and I wanted to count every freckle scattered across her nose and cheeks. I could barely think over the sound of my pulse pounding. When she leaned forward and pressed a kiss in the divot at the base of my throat, it felt like a drop of lava. The heat of it slid directly into the liquid need humming through me. The threads of desire were spinning tighter and tighter inside.

Luna leaned back, lifting her head and taking another step closer. It felt as if a force field was vibrating around us. She blinked, drawing my gaze to her thick lashes and the way they curled against her cheeks. I wanted to tangle my hand in her hair and kiss her. I needed something I couldn't even define, but it was all wrapped up in Luna.

Her breasts rose to press against my chest with her breath as her hand slipped around the back of my neck to pull me closer. Our kiss was a brushing, slow touch at first. When she sighed against my lips, I finally gave in, dropping her hand and sliding mine into her curls as I angled my head to the side and claimed her mouth in a deep, devouring kiss.

I had no idea how long that kiss lasted, but it went wild the moment her tongue darted out to meet mine. We took deep sips from each other. I dusted kisses on each corner of her mouth before catching her bottom lip with my teeth and savored the way she let out a needy whimper when I dove back into her mouth.

We finally broke apart and stared at each other. I was tied up in knots, all for her. She blinked before whispering, "Please…"

Chapter Twelve

LUNA

Please...

An electric shock jolted me at that single word. I wasn't one to beg. Ever.

Parker's eyes held mine, dark with need and an intensity of feeling. "As you wish," he whispered.

I felt those words against my lips. His mouth came over mine again, and I loved every second of every kiss. The way his tongue glided against mine, the way he took control without being overpowering, the combination of gentle and commanding.

My knees were weak, and heat suffused me from head to toe. I could feel the slick moisture at the apex of my thighs. We broke apart again, both of us gulping in air. I could feel the hard, hot length of him pressed against my low belly.

I wanted more. I didn't want this to stop, but I

felt as if I were tumbling, as if I couldn't slow down the pace of need galloping through my system. I shocked myself again, reaching between us and boldly stroking over him.

Parker let out a choked sound. "Luna..." He bit out.

"Please," I repeated.

The next span of time was a jumble, a tangle of sensations twined in this fiery yearning. Parker dusted open kisses along my jawline. The graze of his teeth on my neck brought goosebumps rising on my skin in a full-body shiver. A gasp slipped out at the feel of his hand sliding under the hem of my shirt. The calloused surface of his palm sent sparks scattering through me as his touch coasted over my skin, sliding up to cup one of my breasts. His thumb teased over one nipple and then the other.

Everything felt drawn tight inside, to an almost unbearable pressure. The gruff whisper of my name on my skin nearly undid me when I shifted my legs restlessly. His knee slipped between my thighs. I rocked my hips, whispering, "Please," again.

I almost didn't recognize myself in these moments of pleading. Parker lifted his head, his gaze ensnaring mine. "Luna," he rasped, the sound of his voice another match thrown into the fire already snapping and crackling inside. "Are you sure?" he asked.

"Please..." seemed to be the only word I could speak.

His hand slid over my belly, dipping behind the stretchy waistband of my leggings to cup over the damp silk between my thighs. I felt his muttered imprecation against my lips before he pushed that silk out of the way. I let out a ragged cry of relief when his fingers delved into the slippery core of me. He whispered my name again, and I dragged my eyes open. His eyes held mine as his fingers sank into me. "Oh, sweetheart..."

Biting my bottom lip, I chased my release. My breath was coming in sharp pants as my hips rocked into his touch. Everything drew tighter and tighter, to the point I thought I might fly apart. Just when I thought I couldn't take it anymore, when I couldn't bear the pressure, he sank two fingers in deeply as his thumb teased over my clit. The pressure snapped as I cried out, the pleasure breaking through me.

Parker held me close, his arm steadying me around my waist as I trembled all over. I didn't know how long I stood there, all but collapsed against him until he slowly withdrew his fingers and tidied my clothes. My head had fallen into the curve of his shoulder, my palm gripping around his waist where I could feel the banded flex of his muscles.

I wanted more, but somehow, I sensed, for tonight, Parker was not going to give me more. I lifted my head, leaning back slightly.

Before I could say anything, he said, "Even if you ask for more, not tonight." His tone was firm, as if he was trying to convince himself.

My lips curled in a smile. "I thought so."

His gaze sobered as he lifted a hand to slide his fingers through my curls. "I like you, Luna. A lot." His tone was somber, almost reverent.

My heart thumped with a resounding kick of recognition against my ribs. "I like you too," I whispered. "A lot." I tried to gather my thoughts. "What now?"

PARKER

Although it took every ounce of willpower I had not to lift Luna into my arms and cart her upstairs into her bedroom, I didn't. I kissed her once more and physically forced myself to step away. She asked if she could see Fuzzy soon, so we planned a hike. I barely remembered what I said as I left with my body humming from such a rush of need I couldn't think.

After I got home, I resorted to finding my release in the shower. Desperate times, desperate measures, and all that. I fell asleep with Luna swirling in my thoughts. I couldn't help but wonder why I wanted so much with her. I was allergic to commitment, or that's what I had always told myself.

———

"Parker!" My dad's greeting was so loud that I had to pull the phone away from my ear for a second.

"Hey, Dad," I replied with a chuckle. "How are you?"

"Amazing!" he boomed. "I'm in love!"

Another chuckle rustled in my throat. My dad was like a little kid with his rekindled relationship. His youthful enthusiasm was heartwarming. Although I was bemused by it, I knew it was hard won. He had walked a gauntlet of substance abuse and years of reckless decisions to reach a point where he had enough wisdom to make better choices. For the last few years, he had stayed out of jail and stayed sober. He'd stopped trying to make a quick buck and find a shortcut in life.

"I'm happy for you, Dad." I meant every word down to my bones.

I could hear the seriousness in his voice. "I know you are. You know, you could fall in love," he said, so earnestly it twisted my heart.

When it came to making halfway decent choices, my life had been more of a rip the bandage off approach. I'd made my stupid choices that had given me a brutally quick course in what I didn't want from life. And yet, I didn't know how to tell my dad I wasn't so sure love was on the table for me.

Although the mere mention of the word love conjured the feel of Luna in my arms and her big eyes blinking up at me. If there was anyone I could fall in love with, it would be Luna. Panic spun in my chest when I contemplated that. My fear of abandonment was so big inside it felt all-encompassing. Between my mom bolting from my life and my dad bouncing in and out of jail, trust didn't come easy. Not so much in people specifically, but more in the universe and in believing things could work out.

I played it cool and laughed. "You never know how things are gonna work out, Dad. Based on your life, it seems like everything works out when the time is right."

My dad's soft laugh filtered through the phone. "True enough, but you don't have to screw up for as long as I did," he pointed out.

"Dad, I love you, and I'm always glad to talk to you. You know that, but let's not make every call about how I should fall in love and get married."

His laugh was wry. "I'm just calling to check in. Tell me what's new."

Yet again, my thoughts spun toward Luna. She was the equivalent of the North Star in my brain lately. If I told my dad a single thing about Luna, he'd be all over my case about her.

"Not a whole lot. Livin' life," I replied vaguely.

I rolled my truck to a stop in the parking lot at Firehouse Café and tapped the button to turn the engine off. "Stopping to get some coffee, like I do most days. This afternoon, I'm taking Fuzzy for a hike."

"How is that guy?" my dad asked.

"He's good. You know Fuzzy, he's easy come, easy go with life. So when did you say you're gonna be nearby for your honeymoon?"

"Well, we're doing that ferry trip soon, so I'll text you the dates."

"As long as we don't get called out to a fire, I'll be here. You know we're in fire season, so that could happen."

"Oh, I know."

"Well, what's up with you, Dad? I mean, aside from love and all that."

"I'm doing good. Going to my NA meetings, loving life with my lady."

"It's always good to hear from you, Dad. Love you and talk to you soon, okay?"

"You know it. Love you too." I ended the call, smiling as I climbed out of my truck.

In spite of everything, I'd never for a second doubted my dad loved me. When I was a kid, my dad had a clumsy emotional quality. As if he wasn't sure how to get it right. Older and wiser now, I understood there was no getting everything right in life. He'd fumbled his way through.

"Parker!" a voice called as I approached the door to the café.

Turning, I grinned, calling, "Hey!"

As my friend Hudson approached, he pocketed

his keys when he reached my side. "What are you up to today?"

"Getting coffee and hopefully a donut."

Hudson clapped me on the shoulder as we turned and continued walking in together. It would always amaze me that we'd met in detention, become best friends, lost touch, and reconnected years later. Life was funny sometimes. It spun in different directions. Sometimes mistakes could be the best thing that ever happened when you took the lesson offered from them.

I couldn't help the anticipation that began to buzz through my veins when we got in line at the counter. Luna wasn't always here, but she was often here. Even though we'd made plans for the hike today, I didn't know if she'd be here. Disappointment gusted through me when we got to the front of the line and she wasn't there.

Hudson immediately asked, "How fresh are the donuts?"

Casey grinned. "An hour, and there's only four left. You'd better get them now because Luna's left for the day."

"Give me all four," Hudson said quickly.

I elbowed him in the side. "I'd like one."

He rolled his eyes. "Fine, Parker can have one."

Casey giggled as she reached into the display case. When Hudson stepped away to go to the restroom while she made our coffees, she caught my eye. "So, I have one thing to say."

"Uh, okaaay," I said slowly.

"You be good to Luna. She told me she's going on a hike with you and Fuzzy today." Casey's gaze bordered on stern.

I had so many questions, but there were customers in line behind me. "Of course, I'll be good to Luna. Do I need to worry about what she's saying about me?"

One of Casey's brows arched up. "Maybe, maybe not. You only need to worry if you're not good to her." At that, she handed me my coffee.

———

"Okay, dude, you need to be on your best behavior."

Fuzzy looked up at me with his soulful brown eyes. Whether he understood me or not, he butted his head gently against my knees. He bounded outside, leaping into the front of my truck a moment later, his tail swishing against the seat.

A short drive later, I parked in front of Luna's house. The hum of anticipation was getting louder in my body. I had wondered about Luna, who I'd thought of as Jane, for years. That afternoon on the beach had almost seemed like a mirage afterwards, as if it hadn't really happened.

I'd always hoped I'd see her again. When I didn't

for so many years, that afternoon felt like a blip. I hadn't ever considered being serious with someone, then or now. Yet, I'd connected with her so easily that day. Afterwards, I'd talked myself out of it, convincing myself it had been a fluke, that my mind was playing tricks on me.

And yet now, I knew it hadn't been a fluke. Although my mind wanted me to shy away, my heart wanted a chance with her. A real one.

Fuzzy recognized where we were and raced out of my truck with sheer excitement. His entire body was vibrating when we stood in front of Luna's door. I glanced down, chuckling as I knocked. When Luna opened the door, Fuzzy immediately began circling her legs and letting out these little happy yips.

She knelt down to pet him. "Fuzzy!" she enthused.

He licked her face, turning in a tight circle in front of her. She glanced up at me. "I suppose I could greet you. Hello," she offered.

"Priorities," I teased. "I'm glad Fuzzy's so happy to see you."

A moment later, she straightened, glancing down at her shirt. "I'm covered in dog hair."

"Welcome to my life," I said dryly.

"Are you ready to go?" she asked.

"Fuzzy certainly is." He was poised at the top of

the steps to her porch, intently studying a squirrel climbing a tree.

Luna smiled. "I'm ready to go. Let me just grab my phone and my keys."

A moment later, we were walking down the steps. "This way." She gestured.

I followed her around the back of her house to the same path we'd taken the other day. "It's nice you're so close to this trail network," I commented, idly spinning Fuzzy's leash in a circle as we walked.

"I love it. I usually get out for a hike at least once a week. Have you seen that viewing spot that looks out over the valley? It's a great place to watch the sunset or sunrise."

Nodding, I replied, "It's where I usually hike to with Fuzzy. So how did you luck into this place?"

"It's my grandmother's. She has a larger house nearby, and she used to rent this out. After I worked some in Juneau and finished my culinary program last year, she told me I could stay here. Sometimes I worry she's losing out on the rent money. I pay rent even though she says I don't have to."

"It's a nice little place."

"It's perfect for me," Luna replied.

We fell quiet once the path from her house connected with the main trail. The main trail led to a network of smaller trails that all circled back. I unclipped Fuzzy's leash. He liked to bound ahead and loop back and was good about staying nearby.

Walking through the trees reminded me of why I'd loved those hours with Luna that single afternoon a decade ago. It was simply comfortable to be with her. I didn't feel the need to fill any quiet spaces. Perhaps the phrase "in companionable silence" was trite, but it was meaningful. Experiencing it felt like falling into a pocket of ease, a place I could stay forever.

The moment my mind formed the word "forever", I shied away from it. Permanent wasn't something I contemplated when it came to relationships. My life had taught me that forever wasn't something that existed for me.

Fuzzy led the way, veering up to the viewing point all on his own. Luna glanced over at me, her curls bouncing in her ponytail. "He knows where to go."

I chuckled. "That he does. We've been here a few times. I like this trail because it's not too long, but it's beautiful. When I need to get him out for some exercise, we usually come here."

"Does he like to fetch?"

"If you get a ball out, he'll play fetch with you for hours," I offered with an emphatic nod.

Luna's giggle cinched around my heart. "If he ever stays with me when you're out of town, I will make sure that I have plenty of balls for him to fetch."

"I was serious when I said I'd love for you to take

care of him."

She glanced up again. "Really?"

I couldn't even stay on topic. "To be honest, I've had a crush on you ever since I met you." Hearing myself speak the blunt truth startled me. Pink crested high on Luna's cheeks. I gave my head a little shake. "That didn't answer your question. My job means I need someone to take care of him when I'm out of town. He likes you. I always figure it out, but I'm serious. I'd love for him to stay with you. I'll pay you."

Luna's eyes went wide. "You don't need to pay me! I love dogs. I never got to have one growing up. You do *not* need to pay me. Just give me a call when you need to leave for work, and I will come get Fuzzy."

My chest felt a little funny, as if my heart itself had stumbled and fallen. Luna threw me off-balance emotionally, discombobulating me so thoroughly that I was constantly trying to reorient myself.

A moment later, Fuzzy rounded a curve in the path, and we followed him to where the view opened wide. A beautiful valley stretched in front of us. In the distance to one side, you could see the ocean, an inlet from the Pacific Ocean that led to Anchorage. To the other side, the mountains were a tall, commanding presence against the sky.

With it being late autumn, the snow was dusting

the mountains. Luna took a quick breath, letting it out in a happy sigh. "I love it here."

I glanced down at her. "It's beautiful."

"Before you moved here to work on the hotshot crew, had you ever been to Willow Brook?" she asked.

I shook my head. "Nope. I bounced around with my dad, but it was mostly in the Southeastern part of the state, Juneau, Fireweed Harbor, Skagway, and so on, in that little stretch. A few times, we came to Anchorage for shopping. Once, we moved to Fairbanks for a fresh start. While I'm used to winter, Fairbanks is fucking cold."

Luna threw her head back with a laugh, the sound echoing out over the valley. When her gaze leveled with mine again, her eyes were twinkling. "Fairbanks *is* fucking cold. We went there one winter. My parents wanted to produce "content" of us doing the RV thing in the winter. It was so cold and dark." She rolled her eyes. "We ended up leaving within a few weeks, but we had to do enough videos for three whole months of content. It wasn't fun."

When I thought about my childhood, which was no walk in the park, it seemed downright stable compared to that. Luna's life just went to show that there were different kinds of chaos. While Dad hadn't been what I'd call stable, he'd been loving, if uncertain and sometimes confused about parenting and life. I remembered when I was an adult and ran into one of my teachers from middle school. She'd shared that he used to go to my parent-teacher conferences and earnestly ask for advice on how to respond to behavioral issues with me. She'd told me he was a sweet guy, even if, in her words, he didn't always make the best choices. If that didn't sum my dad up, not much else did.

Unsure of what to say to Luna, I gathered my thoughts. "Well, that doesn't sound great."

Luna shrugged. "I didn't mean to make that moment awkward."

Turning to face her, I reached for her hands. "Luna, you didn't make the moment awkward. I think we covered awkward at dinner the other night, right?"

Her lips twisted to the side before she smiled sheepishly. "I guess so."

I could sense she didn't want to keep talking about her parents. "Maybe someday you and your parents can build a relationship that feels better."

She blinked before her curls bounced with her nod. "I hope so. I know they love me, it just feels like they got caught in this cycle where they kept thinking something would break through and make it all worth it." She squeezed my hands. "Thank you."

"For what?"

"Understanding." She startled me when she leaned up and pressed a kiss on the side of my jawline. That brief touch felt like a lick of fire, the heat flickering outward.

I wasn't thinking when I took a step closer and palmed her cheek, enchanted just to be with her. "I'm more glad than you can ever know that I found you again."

Luna's eyes widened slightly before she whispered, "I am too."

I was lost in her gaze through several echoing beats of my heart. With every second, it felt as if the connection between us was tightening, stitching our bond tighter and tighter.

On the heels of a breath, I dipped my head and fit my mouth over hers. I slid my hands around to cup her nape and kissed her as if she were the very air I needed.

Chapter Fourteen

LUNA

My body molded against Parker, with one of my arms banded around his waist and my other palm sliding up his chest, savoring the muscled planes. I wanted to climb him like a tree. At the sound of Fuzzy's bark, I snapped out of the haze.

We broke apart abruptly, both of us glancing toward Fuzzy, who was looking out over the valley. In the distance, a large bull moose was walking through the tall grass. Beyond that, a grizzly bear appeared to be grazing on something. I wasn't great at judging distance, but I guessed, as the crow flew, the bear was maybe a mile away.

Alarm jolted through me. "We should go!"

Parker nodded. "I absolutely agree." He snapped his fingers, and Fuzzy trotted right over. "Let's go."

Having grown up traveling all over Alaska, I'd

seen my share of brown bears and grizzly bears. I always preferred to be a comfortable distance away. I was relieved that Parker seemed to be on the same page. He clipped Fuzzy on his leash and kept a firm hold of my hand as we walked at a brisk pace back down the trail.

Relief rolled through me once we were inside my house. I took a deep breath and let out a heavy sigh. "Okay, we're here. Hopefully, the bear didn't follow us."

Parker flashed a grin. "I think we're in the clear. When I'm close to town, I tend not to think about bears and wildlife much, but wildlife is everywhere in Alaska."

"I have a love-hate thing with wildlife. I love feeling a part of nature, and I respect it. I also don't ever want to get attacked by a bear."

Parker chuckled, and the sound sent a shiver through me, making my belly spin in a dizzying flip. I tore my gaze away from his and glanced at the clock above the stove in the kitchen. "We talked about hiking, but we didn't talk about whether we were doing anything else. Do you want some dinner?" Evening was approaching. "We could get takeout somewhere, and then I'll make dessert."

"I can't say yes fast enough," Parker said, his lips kicking up at one side in a lopsided grin. My belly went to spinning all over again.

———

I filled a bowl of water for Fuzzy, watching as he lapped it up quickly, his tail wagging in joy when he looked back up at me.

"So, um…" I paused, feeling a little anxious as I rested my hand on the edge of the counter and looked over at Parker. "We can get takeout from the Gallery Café."

Parker shrugged. "I will honestly eat anything. I like pizza, I like the Gallery Café, I like Wildlands. I also like the new brewery restaurant."

"Oooh! Let's do that," I replied.

"Sounds like a plan. I'm actually going to need to stop by my place to feed Fuzzy. Should we order, and then I'll pick it up on the way back?"

"Works for me. If you want, I can ride along with you."

"How about you look up the menu on your phone while I drive? I'm sure Fuzzy will let you ride in the front," he teased a few minutes later as we approached his truck.

Fuzzy was trotting between us, his tail swinging when I glanced down at him. "Is there room for him in the back?"

Parker's truck had one of those extra cab spots with a small door. Parker chuckled as he held the door open for Fuzzy. "There's plenty of room for him in the back. He can even lie down. I have blankets and everything. When he wants to stretch out when I'm driving on longer trips, this is where he likes to nap."

Fuzzy happily hopped in the back. As soon as I climbed in the front, he gave me a slobbery kiss on my ear. I laughed as Parker handed me a napkin. "He does that."

After Parker had started driving, I perused the menu for the new winery and brewery restaurant on my phone. "I've only been out here once, have you been?"

"Oh yeah. It's like the place in Fireweed Harbor where I spent a few years growing up. That restaurant's been in that town for decades."

I ordered the halibut tacos with mango salsa while Parker opted for a salmon burger. A few minutes later, Parker came to a stop in front of a row of three small houses situated amidst a stand of trees.

"These are cute!" I glanced toward him.

"I'm assuming you know Josie," he said. "She sometimes works at Firehouse Cafe."

"Of course I know Josie! I knew her when I was little before we moved away, and I see her at least once a week at the cafe."

"Her boyfriend, Tate, owns these and rents them out. When I accepted the firefighter position here, he hooked me up. You can come in if you want. Fuzzy isn't due for dinner for another hour, but I need to get his food. I try to keep him on a schedule."

My curiosity led me to follow him into his small house. It had a cute little front porch and a peaked roof with a bright red stainless-steel roof.

After we walked inside, I glanced around the open layout downstairs with a living room and kitchen. Parker gestured in a circle. "This is it, there's a bathroom and laundry to the side and then —" His arm swung over toward the stairs. "A bedroom upstairs with another bathroom. Tate could make some serious cash if he rents these during the busy season, but he insists he wants to make them available for long-term tenants."

"Tate seems like a good guy. Do you see him and Josie much?"

Parker chuckled as he fetched a bag of dog food and some treats out of a kitchen cabinet. "All the time. They live right next door, and he works with me."

A few minutes later, we were driving out toward Fireweed Winery & Restaurant. "What made you want to be a firefighter?" I asked as he drove.

When I glanced his way to see his arm resting on the steering wheel with his hand dangling over it, my eyes lingered on the subtle flex of his forearm as he steered. Heat spun through my veins, and I forced my eyes away as he replied, "When my probation officer set me up with a vocational program, this was the only thing interesting to me. I love it. It's never boring."

I glanced over when he chuckled. "I imagine not. How often do you travel in the summer?"

"It varies. I imagine we'll get called out soon. When I first trained, there weren't as many wildfires, but now they're a lot more frequent. Alaska is busy, along with other areas. If we're not dealing with fires here, we rotate with other crews anywhere we're needed."

Anxiety twisted through me as I contemplated him out in the wilderness, fighting literal fires. "Do you worry about your safety much?"

Parker's eyes flicked to mine before briefly stating, "Of course I do. Statistically speaking, just driving down the highway carries more risk than firefighting."

I let out a little snort. "I suppose."

We fell quiet when he turned onto the road that led to the winery. This was a beautiful part of town with a view of fields with the mountains in the distance. Of course, the mountains were always in the distance in Alaska. Alaska was a show-off when it came to nature.

After we ate, Parker insisted on paying for our dinner. When I tried to argue the point, he arched a brow. "Luna, you're making dessert, and I have absolute confidence it's gonna be amazing."

Heat blazed in my cheeks as he parked in front of my house. "You have a lot of confidence."

He tapped the button to turn the engine off before leaning over and surprising me with a quick and fierce kiss. "I've had your donuts. I know how good they are."

I was so flustered that I fumbled to unbuckle my seatbelt.

Chapter Fifteen

PARKER

"Amazing. I told you." I finished my first bite of Luna's strawberry rhubarb crumble cake. She'd whipped it up within minutes after we arrived.

Luna bit her lip, pink flaring on her cheeks as she looked over from across her small kitchen table. "Told me what?"

"That this would be amazing." I took another bite, closing my eyes as I savored the subtle sweet flavor with bursts of tartness from the berries and rhubarb.

She pressed her lips together. "Thank you," she finally said. "I love to bake."

"Good thing because you're seriously skilled. I'm decent in the kitchen, but that's it. I definitely can't bake donuts or anything like this magic." I gestured toward the baking pan in the center of the table.

Fuzzy was sound asleep on the floor beside Luna's feet. I didn't doubt my dog's love for me, but I was pretty sure that he thought Luna was the best human being in the universe. While we were waiting for the crumble cake to finish baking, she'd whipped up molasses oatmeal dog biscuits for him. He'd gobbled two of them in quick succession before she put the others away, assuring him he could have more later.

Everything about today felt too good to be true. Time and again, it harked me back to that feeling from that afternoon. Over the years, I convinced myself those hours were better in my memory than they'd been in real life. But now, I was pretty sure my memory didn't do the time justice. There was a comfort and an ease to sharing space with Luna. I now thought of her in my memory as Luna. Because that name suited her in a way that Jane never had.

It was approaching the time where I should make a graceful exit, but I didn't want to leave. Yet again, a comfortable silence fell between us.

I felt her gaze on me and lifted mine to hers. "You look like you're thinking a little too hard, Luna," I teased lightly.

She was quiet for a beat. "I don't want you to leave tonight." Her words came out in a rush, followed by a wash of deep pink staining her cheeks. "I shouldn't have said that," she added quickly.

"I definitely don't want to leave." I was completely serious. "So I'm really glad you said that."

She smiled sheepishly as she looked over at me. "Well, good then. At least we agree."

A little later, Luna was trying to keep me from washing the dishes. "Luna, you baked," I protested. "And it was amazing. It's a total of four plates."

"And the bowl." She pointed to the large mixing bowl she'd used.

I chuckled and kept on cleaning up. After I finished, for the first time, awkwardness hung in the air. I knew what I wanted, although it wasn't defined. I didn't have to have everything now with Luna. I simply didn't want to leave. I wanted to stretch this time with her further.

She twisted the dish towel between her hands nervously until I reached for it. "What are you worried about?"

She took a quick breath, straightening her shoulders. "I really like you, Parker, and I'm afraid I'm going to screw this up."

"You can't screw this up, Luna. I really like you too."

The sound of her quick inhalation was audible. She startled me just like she had the other night. She tossed the dish towel on the counter and closed the distance between us. Seconds later, she was leaning up to kiss me.

The moment our lips collided, fire blazed

through me, and my mind went blank. There was a sweetness, a pure quality to her that stripped away my defenses and knocked me to my knees inside. She kissed me boldly, her tongue tangling with mine briefly before we broke apart.

We stared at each other, our breath heaving together. I scrambled inside, frantically trying to get purchase, trying to steady myself internally. The fierce need I felt for Luna was more powerful than any I'd experienced and tested all of my discipline.

"I want you, Luna." My voice was decisive, the edges of my words scuffed from the force of my need.

I closed my eyes to gather myself. After several deep breaths, I leveled my gaze with hers.

She stared back at me, lifting her chin slightly and squaring her shoulders. "I want you, Parker."

I swallowed. "I don't want to rush this," I finally said.

Luna meant too much to me. What she represented in my memory and in my heart was, not to be trite, something special. There weren't many people I felt like I could be truly myself with. She was on that very short list. I trusted her on a bone deep level.

"I don't know that we can rush anything. We've already blown past all of it." She straightened up even further. "I'm halfway to falling in love with you, and I can't believe I just said that out loud, but it's true."

My heart practically cracked a rib. My voice was raspy when I replied, emotion crashing through me so fast my throat felt tight. "I'm halfway in love with you. But—"

Luna stepped closer, placing her palm on my chest, where my heart felt pulled toward it, as if she were a magnet.

"I feel like we lost so much time," Luna said. "I don't want to miss any more."

As I stared into her eyes, I felt like I understood something even if she wasn't saying it explicitly. She had missed so many things once her parents went on the road and turned her life into a display of video clips curated and fed to the masses. She didn't want to miss any of the real parts of life. This, between us, was achingly real.

I placed my hand over hers, curling my fingers around it. "Okay. Here's the thing, I want you so bad. I want it all. At any second, if you decide you want to slow down, all you have to do is say so."

Her lips curled in a slow smile, joy and passion sparking in her eyes. "I don't think that's going to happen, but okay. The same goes for you," she said earnestly.

I chuckled. "Luna, I waited years hoping I'd see you again. And then, I finally did. Pretty sure that's not gonna happen for me either, but I appreciate you making sure I know."

When she giggled, the sound slipped through the defenses around my heart, curling up in a corner. Warm and safe. The way my heart felt in her hands.

Luna turned her hand to lace her fingers with mine before stepping back and tugging me away. "The kitchen is great now, but..." she teased as she pulled me through the living room over to the stairs.

I took a quick glance over at Fuzzy. He was out for the count, snoring softly, where he slept on the kitchen floor.

"Do you need to take Fuzzy out?" Luna asked, stopping at the base of the stairs.

"No, he should be good. I took him out for a break before we started cleaning up. I was just making sure he was good and asleep."

She giggled again. "He looks very asleep."

A laugh rumbled in my throat as I squeezed her hand. "He's a really good sleeper."

I followed when she began walking up the stairs. A sense of anticipation began drumming through my body. My entire focus was on Luna. I barely registered that the stairs came to a landing with a single door that led into a large bedroom. The bed suited Luna perfectly. It was a tall four-poster bed with pillows piled high and light, silky fabric draped over the posts.

Luna stopped in front of it, dropping my hand

and turning to face me. When she looked up at me, she looked hesitant with trepidation flickering in her gaze.

"If you've changed your mind —" I began.

She shook her head quickly. "I haven't changed my mind, but I'm nervous to tell you something. I'm afraid, when I do, that you'll change your mind."

"Luna, that's not possible," I said flatly.

She studied me, and I swore it felt like she was reaching into my heart. She took a deep breath and squared her shoulders. "I'm a virgin," she said so quickly I almost didn't catch it.

"What?" I shook my head, almost as if to myself.

She let out a sigh of frustration. "I'm a virgin." This time, her words were slower and clear. "And it's stupid. I think that whole thing is stupid, women saving themselves, or men thinking they're getting some prize. It's so ridiculous. But thanks to my parents, even though my whole life was plastered on an online family influencer channel, I didn't have a regular adolescence. I didn't have a boyfriend. I didn't even want to date because I didn't want to end up being the subject of some kind of commentary. Since I moved away..." She shrugged and rolled her eyes again. "Well, it's just weird."

Once again, Luna left me reeling. Intellectually, I understood all of her points and, I suppose, agreed with them. Fuck me. "Luna, are you sure you're ready for this?"

"Oh, my God!" Hands on hips, she narrowed her eyes. I shifted on my feet. "I'm almost thirty years old. And everything I said about how I feel about you is true. Can you just not have it be a whole thing? I thought about not even telling you because I don't think it's that important. You were the first guy I kissed, but you're not the only guy I've kissed. I just haven't wanted things to go further. Some people suck at kissing." She pursed her lips as if she'd eaten something bitter. "I really like kissing you."

Luna's openness and vulnerability twisted my heart. Much as part of me wanted to bolt because this felt like far more than I bargained for, that wasn't fair and I knew it.

"I really like kissing you too." *Obvious, much?* my mind taunted me.

"Are you going to freak out and tell me we can't do this then?" The annoyance in her tone elicited a chuckle.

"I understand your point, logically, but I don't want to screw up."

She flung a hand in the air. "That's impossible. Everything you do feels good." When Luna stepped closer and placed her palm on my chest, and whispered, "Please," I was lost.

To her. To this. To us.

Although, I suppose my heart had been lost to her since that afternoon on a beach all those years ago when I thought her name was Jane and she had straight hair. Her curls were my favorite thing about her, beyond simply who she was as a human being.

I sucked in a gulp of air. "What I said earlier stands." I opened my mouth to repeat myself, but Luna rolled her eyes.

"I know, I know. If I change my mind at any point, all I have to do is say so. Yep. Got it." She circled her hand in the air impatiently. "Now, can we get with the program, please?"

A laugh slipped out when she leaned up to kiss me again. The feel of her lips, warm and soft against mine, was enough to make me forget everything but how much I wanted her and how good it felt to kiss her.

LUNA

The next span of time passed in a blur of sensation. Parker's tongue teasing mine. His teeth catching my bottom lip and tugging it lightly. Hot kisses dusted on the corners of my lips. His mouth blazing a trail of open kisses on the side of my neck while I trembled and shivered against him.

I felt as if I were melting inside, with sparks flickering everywhere, sending sensations in shivering waves through me. It all felt too powerful to contain. I was restless and needed more. When we broke apart between kisses, I stepped back and yanked my shirt off.

When I glanced toward Parker, his eyes were wide. "What?" I pressed.

"Luna," he began before pausing to take a rough breath. "We don't have to rush."

My hands stilled from unbuttoning my jeans. "I know. But I want to feel you."

The sound of his swallow was audible in the room, followed by his breath sucking in between his teeth. I didn't wait and shoved my jeans down, kicking them free. I tossed my bra to the side and was just about to hook my fingers over my panties when Parker caught one of my hands in his.

"I need you to slow down." His voice was taut.

I lifted my eyes to his. "Okay, but you need to take your shirt off. Actually, you need to strip down to catch up to me."

Parker let out a choked laugh. "Deal." The seconds ticked by as he took his T-shirt off and kicked his jeans to the side. My belly swooped as I studied him. I knew he was fit, but I'd been unprepared for *this*.

Parker was pure muscle, his shoulders broad, his chest muscled planes with a dusting of dark hair that narrowed down over his defined abs. His fitted boxer briefs molded to his strong thighs. My eyes trailed along a scar over his rib cage and another on the outside of his knee.

I closed the distance between us, tracing my fingertips over one scar and then the other. His breath hissed through his teeth again. "What happened?" I lifted my eyes to his. There was a subtle flush high on his cheekbones, and his eyes were dark.

He pointed to his side, where my fingertips

rested lightly. "Cut myself on a branch. No big deal." Gesturing to his knee, he added, "That was a mean rock. I've been lucky."

"These happened when you were fighting fires?"

He nodded as he turned slightly. My eyes landed on a jagged scar on the side of his back. A surprised gasp escaped. My fingertips traced along the angry scar.

"What happened?"

"That was a burning branch dragged across my back." He turned back around. "That's it. Other than a few bruises here and there, but those fade."

My palm fell to his chest, gratified to feel the rapid drumbeat of his heart. "I know you love your job," I said softly, "but I want you to be safe."

He curled his hand over mine, his gaze intent. "I'm safe. I promise."

My hand fell away as he stepped closer and cupped my cheeks as he brought his lips to mine, once again claiming my mouth in a devouring kiss. Parker's kisses made my thoughts go up in smoke. Finally, the sensation I'd been craving, the feel of my skin pressed against his, was a full body experience. The subtle prickle of the hair on his chest brushing my breasts drew my nipples to tight points.

His palm slid down to curl around my waist, and I felt the hard length of him pressed against the soft curve of my belly. The sensation between my thighs was liquid and slick. I whimpered into our kiss as his tongue tangled with mine before we broke apart. We were both gasping for breath.

"Luna," he rasped.

"What?" I whispered.

"I want to take this slow, but I'm not sure I can."

We were pressed tightly together, and I could feel my heart racing along with his. "It's okay. I'm in a hurry too," I said fervently.

His lips curled at the corners in the barest hint of a smile before he nudged me back with a knee, and my hips bumped against the back of my bed. One kiss melted into the next, his lips blazed a burning path down my neck. He teased my breasts, sucking one nipple in and then the other. The sensation of his teeth grazing over them drew a sharp cry from me as the feeling sizzled right to my core.

I was restless, needy, and begging. "Parker, please..."

"Right here, sweetheart," he murmured against my belly as he levered me back.

He dusted hot kisses on the inside of my thighs, and I was trembling as his fingertips trailed over my panties.

I was generally practical when it came to clothes, but I loved silk and lace panties. The silk was so wet that it clung to me. He muttered something against my thigh, and I cried out when he pushed the silk to the side and teased his fingers through my drenched folds. He murmured something that I could've sworn was, "Oh, fuck me."

"You could do that," I hopefully answered.

Parker chuckled as he lifted his head with a ragged breath. Alarm bolted through me when he started to move away. He snagged his jeans off the floor, reaching for his wallet. When he started striding back, he had a condom packet in hand.

He tossed it on the bed beside me. "Thinking ahead," he explained.

I reached out, sliding my hand over the ridge of his arousal. He closed his eyes. I decided to take matters into my own hands, literally. Curling my hands over the edge of his boxers, I tugged them down over his thighs swiftly. I was feeling entirely inexperienced, having never made it all the way, so to speak. When I saw the glistening bead of his arousal, I leaned over and licked it.

Parker let out a guttural groan and began to say something else, but I didn't wait. I leaned forward, closing my mouth over the tip and sucking it in. His fingers laced into my hair, he gripped tightly.

"Luna," he groaned.

I sucked him in, curling my hand around his length as I savored the salty flavor that broke across my tongue. I loved that I could take control like this. Again and again, I sucked him in, stroking my hand up and down his length with each motion. I could feel him beginning to tighten, his body trembling. When he growled my name again and let out a sharp sound, I drew him in once more, taking in his release.

When I leaned back, lifting my eyes to his, he took a shaky breath. "Holy hell," he muttered.

I bit my lip as I smiled up at him, feeling a surge of power that only deepened the arousal inside, spinning into the fiery need snapping and crackling inside of me. The next few moments were rushed.

Parker dragged my panties down, pressing my knees apart as he lifted his eyes to mine, his gaze dark. "Your turn."

More than ready for my turn, I cried out when he brought his mouth to my sex, two fingers sinking into the core of me. Yet again, it was one sensation melting into the next. His tongue teasing me, my channel rippling and clenching around his fingers, a sense of restlessness unspooling inside as I trembled. My hands gripped the comforter, flexing and unflexing, crying his name in ragged gasps. Finally, *finally*, he gave a little pressure right over my clit with his thumb and then sucked it in. The pleasure drew so tight I almost couldn't bear it before it broke through me in piercing rays as I cried out.

Trembling, I watched through heavy-lidded eyes as he rose up, rolling a condom on. He eased me further back onto the bed, whispering, "Are you sure?"

"Hurry."

I savored the feel of his weight coming over me,

the press of his thick crown at my entrance, followed by a slow glide inside and a long pinch of pain. When I tensed, he held completely still. "Are you okay?"

I breathed through it, and my body softened around his length. Curling my legs around his hips, I whispered, "Yes."

His eyes burned into mine. "Hold on, sweetheart."

Chapter Seventeen

PARKER

I could barely breathe. With the feel of Luna's channel clenching around me, her skin soft and damp, I was awash in sensation and lost in the emotion rushing through me. I took several deep breaths, trying to hold still.

She was impatient and rocked her hips toward mine. Yet again, like every moment with her, she held me in thrall. Drawing back, I filled the slick core of her again. I tried to keep my weight off of her, resting on one elbow as we rocked together.

My own release was tightening inside, like a storm building, lightning waiting to strike. But I needed her to find her release again. When I felt her begin to tighten, I shifted slightly, reaching between us and giving a subtle pressure over her swollen clit.

Her eyes went wide, and she cried out my name on the heels of another ragged breath.

Only then did I give in and let the lightning strike. My release slammed through me so hard, my mind filled with static. I held tight until I stopped shuddering. When I could gather myself, I rolled over on my side, where Luna collapsed against me, soft and warm. I liked to think I had some control. I *never* did with Luna.

Eventually, I felt her move, her palm flattening over my heart where it lunged toward her touch. She lifted her head where she had curled it against my neck. I dragged my eyes open to find hers waiting. She looked bright and alert, almost buzzing with energy. Unlike me. I was so overcome with what had passed between us, standing was questionable.

My lips curled into a smile as I slid my hand up her back to sift through her curls. "What is it?"

She kissed me on the cheek, practically beaming as she leaned back. "Thank you."

"Uh, thank you?" I prompted.

Her curls bounced with her nod. "For not freaking out about me being a virgin." She let out a happy sigh. "That was amazing. All of it."

I felt almost goofy as I smiled back at her. "Everything with you is amazing."

I heard the sound of Fuzzy's claws on the stairs. "Incoming," I warned her.

He came into the room and bounded on the bed.

Luna giggled as she turned to look at him. "Should we walk him? Are you okay, Parker?" she finally asked as I tried to dredge up some kind of energy.

I chuckled. "I'm wiped, to be honest. We do need to walk him, but first, we should get dressed."

Luna bounced off the bed while I followed at a much slower pace. She went into the bathroom and looked over at me as I followed her, tossing the condom in the wastebasket by the sink.

"Let's shower, and then we'll walk Fuzzy," she announced.

Showering with Luna almost had me ready to take her all over again. With her skin pink and soap bubbles rolling over it, I loved everything about her and discovered she had more freckles than the ones sprinkled across her nose and cheeks. When I looped my arms around her from behind and dropped a kiss in the curve of her neck as the hot water rolled down over us, the sound of her giggle spun around my heart.

Chapter Eighteen

LUNA

Fuzzy's tail swished against my legs as he circled me excitedly by the door. Glancing over to Parker, I asked, "Does he need to be on a leash?"

Parker shook his head. "I always carry one, but he stays close."

The night air was cool when we stepped outside. With my hair still damp, I shivered a little. Fuzzy paused on the stairs at the top of the porch, glancing back as if asking permission.

Parker gestured ahead. "Do your thing," he said with a chuckle.

We followed Fuzzy off the porch. He walked off, angling to the edge of the trees and promptly taking care of business. As soon as he was done, he came racing back to us.

Fuzzy was so excited when we were back inside,

he bounced up and down and circled me happily. I knelt down to stroke him, and he rested his chin on my shoulder. When I smiled up at Parker, he grinned. "I think you're his favorite."

"He's just excited. I'm new to him."

A little while later, when I drifted into sleep curled against Parker's side with Fuzzy asleep between our feet, I realized this felt better than I could've imagined. Whenever I expected to feel awkward with Parker, it never happened.

The following morning, I woke up to Fuzzy licking my face with his paws on the side of the mattress.

"I'll get him." Parker's voice was gruff from sleep.

"I'll walk out with you." I sat up when I felt him roll away.

The sight of Parker, first thing in the morning, sent my belly into flips. Shirtless with his hair rumpled, well, it was a lot to take in. He flashed me a sleepy smile. "You don't have to."

When his eyes dropped down, heat washed over my skin and my nipples tightened as if waving good morning to him. He closed his eyes, his shoulders rising with a deep breath.

When he opened them again, he chuckled. "Luna, you are a walking distraction for me." He swung his feet off the mattress.

"I'm not walking," I pointed out. I quickly

tugged on a pair of fleece pants and top and followed him down the stairs.

Fuzzy bounded out of the door, pausing briefly to glance at Parker. "Go ahead." Parker gestured forward. We walked down the steps while Fuzzy sniffed along the trees before peeing about four times in a row and spending several minutes to find the right place for phase two.

Parker glanced over at me. "It always takes him a few minutes in the morning. He has to find the exact right spot," he said with a chuckle.

Our breath misted in the chilly morning air. The landscape was coated in frost, glittering where the early rays of the sun cast over it. Parker startled me when he reached for my hand and stepped close, his eyes burning into mine as he murmured, "Good morning," just before he dipped his head to give me a kiss.

The feel of his lips was a hot contrast to the cold air. My entire body felt electrified from the touch. "Good morning," I whispered when he lifted his head.

It felt like my heart was smiling. When Parker's lips kicked up at the corner, my belly shimmied. "I'm really glad I found you again," I added.

The moment was broken when Fuzzy came galloping over, letting out a bark and shimmying between our knees to take part in the embrace. After Parker fed Fuzzy, he tugged me into the shower.

Showering with Parker was pretty much the best thing ever. For one, I got an up close and personal view. Just watching the water roll over his muscled back made my knees weak. When he turned around and lifted his head out of the water to smile at me, I thought I might melt on the spot.

When he kissed me and cupped my breasts, teasing my nipples to aching peaks before he sucked one and then the other into his warm mouth, I braced myself against the tiled wall. A moment later, he lifted his head, saying, "Condom."

We stumbled out of the shower before he lifted my hips onto the bathroom counter and brought his mouth to my sex. A fierce climax echoed through me moments later, my hands clenching the bathroom counter as I trembled all over.

His eyes held mine, a hint of a question there. "We can stop now, if you want."

I shook my head, pulling him closer as he rolled a condom on. His gaze was a flame, joining the one burning in my own heart. When he nudged himself at my entrance, I was impatient and rocked restlessly toward him. He filled me in a slow, deep thrust. There was a twinge of soreness, but I savored the feel of him filling me.

He rocked in deep nudges as my legs dangled down over the edge of the counter, the angle creating an intense friction where we were joined. I was chasing my pleasure with each subtle thrust inside of me. All the while, his eyes held mine, and I couldn't look away. He reached between us, pressing his fingers precisely where I needed them.

My head fell back, and I cried out, shuddering all over as the pleasure broke through me in intense shocks. He said my name, his voice gruff, on the heels of a ragged breath as his hand on my hip tightened. I could feel the shivering tautness before his head fell into the curve of my neck. His breath gusted across my skin.

I loved the feel of him holding me close. I could've stayed like that for hours, but his phone began to ring. I could feel him tense slightly, and he lifted his head, smoothing my hair back before he gave me a lingering kiss. "That's work."

"Work? What do you mean?" I had to gather myself, pulling my thoughts out of the haze.

"That's the ring when we're getting called out," he explained.

"Does this mean you're going out to a fire?"

Chapter Nineteen

PARKER

I kissed Luna fiercely and reluctantly forced myself to break away.

"That means we're going out to a fire."

She blinked, her brow creasing with worry as she whispered, "Okay."

"It's my job."

———

Luna sashayed through my thoughts over the following days. I loved my job. I truly did. The wilderness of Alaska was where I felt most at home. It was nature's cathedral and mine. Whenever I was out in the wilderness, I knew there was something greater than humanity. I felt it in my bones.

When the wind blew, birds called, trees rustled,

and fire blazed, I felt connected to something so much more than myself. I felt like a speck in the universe. I loved that feeling, and I loved my crew. The kinship of being connected to each other and counting on each other, protecting both the wilderness and anyone in harm's way from a fire, was a powerful force.

Even with all of that, for the first time since I'd become a hotshot firefighter, there was an ache in my heart. I missed Luna, something fierce. The memory of that night with her, and those moments before I left, was a warm ember in my heart, something I held onto. Tangled within that was a hint of doubt and worry. Intellectually, I didn't have much faith in the concept of commitment. Not for myself.

Way back when I'd gotten in trouble, my probation officer had set me up with a therapist. That was part of the deal with being on probation and staying out of trouble. My therapist had tried to talk to me about my feelings about my mom, which could be best summed up as "fuck her."

She'd dumped me when I was just a kid. I loved my dad, and he had totally stepped up to the plate. My therapist had gently pointed out that I might have some issues with feeling abandoned and not having faith in others to be there when it mattered. Specifically women, because of what my mom had done.

But this was Luna, the girl I'd met all those years

ago on a pebbled beach in Alaska. I felt safe and comfortable with her. Every time those doubts tried to clamber up and make noise, I swatted them away.

Our crew was dealing with a massive fire that had exploded and grown rapidly in size. Alaska had another dry summer and was still dealing with the aftermath of years of spruce bark beetle kill. Those beetles that had landed in Alaska via overseas shipping and decimated swaths of forest, leaving behind dead trees just waiting to catch fire. We did our best with signs and prohibitions on campfires in certain areas, but people were people. This fire appeared to have been started by some hikers who decided to have a campfire. Nights were cold this time of year, but that was a bad fucking plan.

A branch fell, and I barely dodged it. Glancing over my shoulder, I caught Hudson's eyes. "What the hell, man?" I called, flashing a smile.

We were working our way through, cutting down dead spruce trees. They were dry as a bone. The whole crew was stretched out along this line in the forest. It was a section of the forest that had been logged, probably a few decades prior. This part of Alaska was in the central part of the state. As the crow flew, we were a few hours north of Willow Brook. It was a premier area for hunting and fishing.

Several hours later, with the sound of chainsaws finally off, we gradually made our way to a fire stand. These stands were monitored by volunteers and park staff. An alert volunteer had reported this fire. With most of Alaska sparsely populated, the wilderness was vast enough to get lost in. Beside this outlook post was a convenient cabin, occasionally used for hunting, but for us it was a place to shelter for the night. Between the fire outlook and the cabin, we didn't have to sleep outside.

Although by most standards, the rustic shelter would be considered rough camping. With Graham and Jonah organizing us, we got our gear propped up, checked on the status of our various tools, and plunked down to scramble up some food for the evening.

"What's on the menu tonight?" Griffin asked. He was seated on the ground, leaning against a boulder.

Our crew had a good vibe. Graham and Jonah were superintendents, and they both had an easygoing but authoritative approach. Firefighting took nerve and confidence. Sometimes that meant people being total assholes, but that was not the leadership here. It was organized, confident, and clear. Graham, who'd been superintendent the longest for this crew, didn't tolerate any bullshit. He was respected by all of us, along with Jonah and everyone on the crew.

"We have a pretty good perimeter, so we can use our camp stove," Jonah commented.

Smoke shimmered in a haze in the sky in the distance. We'd been managing this fire for days now. That was the life of a hotshot. We worked collectively with help from planes and helicopters flying above and dropping fire retardant and water. After we'd all tossed out our food options, we settled on freeze-dried mashed potatoes with beef jerky and a dessert of granola bars. Most of us rested against fallen down logs or our packs, chatting casually while we ate.

"Do you know if Tate has any cabins available?" Graham asked me before taking a bite of his granola bar.

I shrugged. "Come winter, the one beside me will be available. Why do you ask?"

Graham thumbed toward Kincaid, one of the newer guys who'd joined our crew. "Kincaid needs a place. He's staying temporarily at one of the short-term rentals through Wildlands, but he needs a longer-term place."

I caught Kincaid's eye. "I'll check on it. Tate says he prefers to do long-term rentals for locals."

Kincaid flashed a smile. "That'd be awesome. Have I met Tate?"

"Maybe? His crew has been out for the last two weeks. This is your first fire with us, right?"

Kincaid nodded. "Yep. Can't beat this view." He lifted his hand, gesturing forward.

"As long as it's not on fire," Jonah chimed in.

I chuckled. "But that's what we do. We make the fire go away and enjoy the view while we're at it." I took a bite of mashed potatoes.

"You know these are damn good." Hudson glanced at me, waggling his brows. "I gotta give you some credit. We went from plain instant mashed potatoes to mashed potatoes with beef jerky and spices."

I grinned. "We need some protein. We worked our asses off today."

Conversation drifted along. When we were offering Kincaid background info on Willow Brook and the surrounding areas, he asked, "So, how bad is winter? People keep warning me to be ready. I'm from Northern Minnesota, so I think I should be able to handle it."

"Oh, you'll be fine," Graham said. "The south-central part of Alaska is no colder than northern Minnesota. We probably get less snow than you did there. Might be a little longer and darker, but it's not like the Northern part of Alaska where they don't see the sun for a few months and it's brutally cold the whole time."

Kincaid snorted. "Yeah, I can do without complete darkness for a few months. I love snow, though. Always have."

"Well, Alaska will give you snow," I commented. "This is the time of year when we should see more northern lights. If we luck out tonight, hopefully we'll get a show."

"What brought you to Alaska?" Hudson asked.

"Aside from the job, I always wanted to see

Alaska. So, I'm here. It's that simple," Kincaid said. "Maybe I should have a more exciting reason, but I figure moving to Alaska is worth it."

"Oh, definitely," Hudson chimed in. "I grew up here, but Alaska is so beautiful it never wears off."

"I completely agree. I feel lucky. Even the flight out to the fire was amazing," Kincaid said.

"Seriously," I said. "Alaska is God's country. Flying over the landscape is mind-blowing."

"Can I bunk up there?" Kincaid thumbed up toward the lookout. The single room was situated on a tall stand with windows on all four sides.

"Go for it. There's enough room for maybe four people to sleep up there. Down here, it'll be crowded, but we can easily fit half the crew in there. Everybody else, we're outside," Graham said with a shrug.

"Should we draw straws?" Hudson quipped.

"I never mind sleeping outside," I offered.

"Same here. Unless it's raining, in which case we're happy because that helps put out the fire," Jonah chimed in wryly.

Cooper plunked down on the ground beside us, returning from a bathroom break. "There's a stream not far away, maybe half a mile. Should we aim for that, for anybody who needs to take a bath?"

"You call that a bath?" Hudson teased.

"I call it less stinky," Cooper replied with a chuckle.

Hudson pulled out his cell phone, eyeing it. "No fucking reception."

"Usually isn't. They don't have a lot of cell towers out here. You missing Stella?" I asked.

Hudson glanced over. "Always. How about you and Luna?"

I glanced over, trying to read his gaze. "What do you mean?"

Leo rolled his head to the side, where he sat nearby with his head leaned against a stack of gear. "Casey," was all he said.

Casey was Leo's girlfriend and one of Luna's good friends. Of course Casey might know what was going on with Luna and me. It was unsettling to feel my heart kick into an unsteady beat. The way I felt about Luna was disorienting. I wasn't used to worrying about someone else, thinking about them and missing them when I was away. At all. In fact, it was safe to say I'd never done that.

"I don't know," I finally replied.

Hudson, who knew me well, narrowed his eyes. "You are freaking out."

"I'm not freaking out," I insisted, wishing my voice didn't sound defensive.

Leo's brows hitched up. "I might not've known you as long as Hudson has, but you seem a little, well, something."

I leaned back, running a hand through my hair and glancing down as it dropped to my lap. There were some scrapes and streaks of soot visible from days of dealing with a fire. "I don't know. I've never been serious about anyone."

"Are you serious about Luna?" Leo asked slowly.

"I guess maybe I'm thinking I might be serious about Luna," I finally said.

Kincaid glanced from me to Hudson to Leo before he shrugged. "I'm the new guy here, but either you're serious about someone, or you're not. I don't know. I'm not prone to giving romantic advice, but you should probably settle on something there."

Hudson snorted a laugh while Leo gave me a knowing grin. "Oh, hell, I like Luna a lot." My heart felt as if the ground underneath it was wobbling.

When I didn't add anything else, Hudson caught my eyes, a sly glint in his. "You'll have to figure that out."

"He's not wrong," Leo said simply.

Not much later, Alaska decided to show off a little more. Although the northern lights mostly occurred when it was colder, from late summer into autumn, there were often gorgeous shows of lights, and tonight gave us one hell of a show.

"Wow," Kincaid commented, his tone reverent.

The sky was shimmering with streaks of pink and purple and silver. It looked as if translucent curtains were ruffling in the breeze as the lights glimmered against the backdrop of a mountain range in the distance with the stars and the moon visible behind the colors.

"Never gets old," Hudson said quietly at my side.

Coming from a life that had filled me with doubt, it was moments like these, out in the wilderness, when I felt most connected to the universe. My dad, definitely not a regular church-going guy, used to joke that his church existed in the trees, the mountains, and the ocean. Whenever the northern lights were showing, he would come wake me up, and we'd sit outside to watch them no matter where we were.

Just now, I felt more settled than I had in a long time, a sense of peace gusting through me like a refreshing breeze. We watched the lights until the brightness started to fade. Coyotes were howling in the distance.

"Think they'll come close?" Kincaid asked.

"We're not their midnight snack, but they might come nose around for food." I chuckled. "They should be pretty well fed this time of year. Early spring, they're a little more reckless."

The guys who were sleeping in the lookout clambered up the ladder, a few others headed into the cabin, and the rest of us stretched out on the ground. We all had enough gear and comfort to keep us warm through cold nights. Even in the summer, it cooled off quick once the sun was gone. The sheer exhaustion of our work knocked me into sleep.

At some point during the night, I woke up and slipped out of my sleeping bag to take a bathroom break a little ways away from camp. Although the fire was in the distance, I could still see the flickering embers in the darkness.

Once I was back in my sleeping bag, I hooked my elbow behind my head and stared up at the stars. Luna sashayed into my thoughts with her riot of curls and her freckled cheeks. I contemplated Kincaid's observation that I should settle on something with my feelings. As Hudson had astutely noted, he wasn't wrong. The problem for me didn't lie within my feelings for Luna, but in my own scarred heart. Getting abandoned by your mother isn't a great feeling, if you didn't know.

When I landed in my dad's world, he somehow instinctively understood he needed to be a balm to the gaping wound in my heart. Maybe things hadn't been the best with him, but from day one, he'd been so enthusiastic to have me there. If he ever got impatient with all the silly things a little boy wanted to do, I never felt it.

It was a contrast to the first years of my life with my mom. My memories were spotty, but it was more a feeling of uncertainty and harshness.

The cutting lesson my mom taught me was not to count too much on anyone, especially on life. Though I didn't doubt the power and depth of my feelings for Luna, it was the very power of them that frightened me. She could hurt me in a way that would cut deeper than anything I'd ever experienced. That was the other lesson of being rejected by one of your parents. It could make you doubt you were worthy. Intellectually, I knew that wasn't how it worked, but it was difficult to talk my heart out of that belief.

When I thought of Luna, my heart wanted to smile because everything about her was good. The muted call of an owl reached me. I fell asleep to thoughts of Luna and wondered if I could give her what she deserved.

Chapter Twenty

LUNA

"You really think I should do that?"

My grandmother blew a puff of air out of her lips, expertly moving a lock of her silver hair out of her eyes. "Of course you should do it."

"You don't seem surprised," I pointed out.

"Janet asked me about it. We are good friends, after all. She thinks of Willow Brook as her family in a way, and you are special to her. She asked me if I thought she should suggest it to you. I think it's perfect. You're about the age Janet was when she started the café. It was right about when—" My grandmother shook her head, her eyes going a little misty. "She married Dan straight out of high school. Young love and all that. He loved being a trucker. When the town decided to build the new fire station and the old building went up for sale, she and

Dan bought it. At the time, we didn't have a single coffee shop in town."

"It's still the only coffee shop in town," I pointed out.

"Exactly why it's a great plan for you to take over." My grandmother beamed at this. "Anyway, she told me she planned to give it to you outright. The building's paid off. She doesn't have any loans on the business. She makes pretty good money. She's only in her sixties, and her health is good. But setting the plan in motion now means she can get you up to speed while she can still work. She doesn't need the money anymore."

Emotion rose inside of me as I looked at my grandmother. "I would love it. You don't feel like it's too much?"

"Luna, honey, Janet loves you. She thinks of you as a granddaughter." Her lips twisted to the side. "She knows you need something for yourself. You've got me, but I'm not getting any younger. Your mom and dad can live their life, but they haven't set up anything to leave to you. You know I have feelings about them choosing to drag you along with them, but that's over. You're an adult now, you've been doing life on your own for a while. You're gonna be okay. All of my property will eventually be yours."

"But I feel like that's too much!" I burst out.

"What's too much?"

"You planning to give me your property, and Janet planning to give me a business!"

My grandmother rolled her eyes. "Luna, you are a hard worker. I don't sleep all that great, so I know you are up and rolling out of that driveway, usually around three or four in the morning, to start baking. I know you don't make a ton of money. You don't ask for a lot. Every single one of your days is a long country mile with that kind of schedule. Life isn't a calculator. Some people get lucky, if you will. That's a privilege. The café will be something you can slip into. But don't fool yourself, you're gonna have to work your tail off."

I didn't feel the tears slipping out until she shoved the stack of napkins in the center of the kitchen table over to me. "I hope those are happy tears."

Laughing softly, I swiped my cheeks and blew my nose. "They are. All right, I'll talk to Janet about it. I want to do it, but I don't want to take anything from her."

"You're not. She's been worrying about this for a while. This will make her feel good about it. She can rest easy. She loves that café. Hell, that café is her baby in a way."

"How come she didn't have kids?" I couldn't help my curiosity.

Sadness passed through my grandmother's gaze. "She had more miscarriages than I think she would want to share. She's well past that stage of life now. That was back in the day when there weren't as many options to help with things like that. She made her peace with it years ago."

"Oh," I said softly. "That must've been hard."

My grandmother nodded, her gaze warm. "Yes, but she made it through. That's one thing getting old teaches you. Hurtful and hard things happen and you keep going. Before you know it, you find a little pocket of peace inside." She was not one to dwell on any topic and moved right along. "Next time you see Janet, let her know you and I chatted about it. This feels new to you, but once you moved back last year, she told me right off she felt like it was for you."

I took a shaky breath, swiping away my tears again. I reached over and grabbed my grandmother's hand, giving it a squeeze. "Thank you."

She squeezed back. "Whatever for, Luna girl?"

"Helping me when I moved away from Mom and Dad. Making sure I had a place to land when I was ready to come to Willow Brook. Pretty much everything." My heart felt like it might crack open from the fullness of emotion inside.

Her weathered face crinkled all over with her smile. "It's called love. You don't need to thank me. Couldn't live with myself if I didn't help you. It's what I wanted to do. It's not even the slightest burden for me."

Chapter Twenty-One

LUNA

"We should get the variety plate platter," Stella announced, closing the menu emphatically.

"Are we getting anything other than appetizers?" Casey prompted.

Madison glanced between them, her lips twitching at the corners. "Stella always wants the appetizer platter."

"Really?" Stella looked surprised, her brows hitching up at the observation.

I leaned over, lightly bumping my shoulder against Madison's. "I've never seen you order anything other than the appetizer platter here. There's absolutely nothing wrong with that."

"I like the variety," Stella explained, just as Tish, Phoebe, Maisie, and Tiffany arrived.

"Let me guess," Tiffany began with a smile as she

sat down beside Stella. "We're talking about the variety platter."

"I can't believe I'm that obvious." Stella shrugged with a sheepish smile.

"It's the easiest option," Casey chimed in. "Trust me on that. I don't cover shifts here anymore, but it's absolutely the easiest thing for waitresses to get a few of those for a group. Otherwise, we're entering long orders, and the kitchen has to deal with them."

We were all on board for the variety platters. After we had ordered our drinks and food, I glanced around the table. "There's a lot of us here tonight," I pointed out.

Maisie leaned back in her chair. "It's because three of the crews are out at fires. That's seventy-five firefighters gone from town."

"That many?" I exclaimed.

"Each hotshot crew has twenty-five firefighters," Maisie explained.

"Do you get updates at dispatch?" I couldn't help but ask.

Casey glanced toward me, a knowing glint in her eyes. "She's wondering because she has a thing for Parker."

My cheeks were burning up. "Casey!"

Unbothered, Casey shrugged, while Maisie laughed softly. "We only get updates at dispatch when they're on the way back or if something happens. For the most part, they're completely out of range. Otherwise, I don't get much information."

Holly arrived with Lucy. They snagged two empty chairs from a nearby table. Holly glanced around once she was seated. "Holy wow. Busy tonight."

After the collective round of greetings, Maisie gestured toward Holly. "She might be the first to get information aside from me."

"About what?" Holly asked.

"Luna has a crush on Parker and was wondering if I got updates when the hotshots are out at fires," Maisie explained nonchalantly.

Holly's blond ponytail swung as she turned to look toward me. "Nate's one of the pilots. You've met him, right?"

"I met him at Firehouse Cafe."

"Oh, that's right. He loves your donuts, by the way," she added.

I felt a little flush of pride at that. It didn't matter how many times people told me they loved my donuts, I loved hearing it. "Thank you. I was just curious about whether anyone knew anything when the firefighters are out in the field."

"I would know when Nate's scheduled for travel for the firefighters, or if he's out working the fire from the air, dropping flame retardant and monitoring. If there's an emergency, and he gets called out early, obviously I'll find out," Holly explained.

I felt Madison's gaze on me and glanced over. "Welcome to loving a hotshot firefighter," she said softly. "You learn to live with the worry."

My heart gave a tricky twist in my chest as I glanced around the table. I knew all of these women, some better than others. Most of them loved firefighters. I let out a sharp sigh. "Well, that sucks," I said flatly.

"Yeah, it kinda does," Lucy chimed in. "You get used to it."

"And when they come home, you can have awesome coming-home sex," Tiffany quipped, and my cheeks burned up all over again.

"How is it going with Parker?" Tish asked.

I paused, considering our last night together. "Good, but—" I took a breath. "I don't know where it's going to go."

Stella looked over at me, her eyes warm. "Hudson thinks Parker's in love with you."

I'd just taken a sip of my water and choked on it, coughing hard enough that Madison helpfully patted me on the back. When I recovered, I looked over at Stella. "What?"

Stella bit her lip to keep from laughing. "That's what Hudson told me. He and Parker are good friends."

"Well, what do you think?" Casey pressed her. "Parker is your brother."

Stella shrugged. "He's my half-brother, but I

didn't know that until over a year ago. I haven't known him long enough to guess if he's in love with Luna, and he hasn't talked to me about it. He also hasn't talked to Hudson about it. It's just what Hudson thinks."

"How did you and Parker connect?" I asked.

"Oh, my mom did this DNA thing, and Parker did too because he suspected he might have siblings through our dad. When my mom and our dad were together the first time, our dad didn't know about Parker because Parker's mom never told him she was pregnant and moved away." Stella's curls swung when she shook her head. "It's complicated. The best summary is young adults being stupid, not using birth control, and having kids."

"Well, okay," I replied with a chuckle.

"Hudson said it's just a gut feeling about Parker loving you," she added.

"Oh." I was trying to contain the burst of joy at that possibility.

"How do you feel about Parker?" Madison asked.

My eyes arced around the big table filled with my friends, some new, some old. Even though part of me felt a little uncomfortable, this was what I had always craved. To have friends. I took a quick breath. "I don't know. I'm not ready to say the word love because that seems really big, but I guess it feels serious."

"How much do you miss him?" Tiffany asked.

"More than I'd like," I said flatly.

"Well, that's a clue," Maisie said. "I can't wait for Beck to get home. I'm used to him being gone because we've been together for years now, but I miss him. I want him home, and the kids miss him."

Conversation meandered along with those who had kids commiserating about juggling everything on their own, while I was busy wondering what it might be like to have a family with Parker. There were so many things that I never really let myself think about. Falling in love, having a committed relationship, having kids, all of those things seemed like asking for too much from the world, so I tried not to hope for much. I didn't trust the universe enough to hand it to me. If I did, the old resentment toward my parents would burn a little hotter inside. I'd missed so many of the milestones while we traveled. No regular school, no friends. It all added up to not trusting the world.

When we were walking out of Wildlands later, Casey stopped with me beside my car. "I hope it's okay that I teased you about Parker." Her brow creased with concern.

"Of course, it is." I paused. "I kind of like being teased by friends. It wasn't something I got to experience much growing up."

Casey threw her arms around me in a big hug, and I savored the feel of it. Her smile was warm as she stepped back. She put her hands on my shoulders, her gaze somber. "Parker likes you. A lot. I don't know if he loves you because, well, I don't know him that well. But have some faith in yourself. You deserve to have good things happen."

"What do you mean?"

Casey's hands fell away as she studied me. "I know we haven't been friends that long, but you're always cheerful and sweet and kind, and I love that about you. You do our tarot card readings, and you kinda have this woo-woo vibe." She giggled a little, drawing one from me. "But it feels like you don't want to ask much from life. You moved away from the whole RV mess." She waved a hand dismissively, annoyance flashing in her eyes. "And, if I ever get the chance, I'll have a word with your parents about what a shitty thing that was, but that's not my point. You don't ever talk about wanting more than what you have. Maybe it *is* enough, but you can fall for a guy. Until I met Leo and sorted out everything that happened to my sister, just being somewhere and kind of hiding away was all I wanted from the world. I didn't let myself want more. You can want more. You are an awesome human being. I think you're falling pretty hard for Parker, and I think that's amazing. Whether it's Parker or something else in your life, don't be afraid to hope for more."

Tears wicked up into my eyes, with emotion tight in my throat as I stared at my friend. "Thank you," I whispered.

She gave me another fierce hug and blew me a kiss before she climbed into her car.

I went home that night, questions swirling in my thoughts. Casey's point was spot-on. I didn't dare ask for more from life. Maybe it was because I didn't even have my own bedroom in the RV. Just having my own space felt like an incredible luxury.

When I got home, Fuzzy greeted me joyously. Dog sitting was the best.

"What do you think, Fuzzy?" I asked a little while later while I rested against my pillows, and he curled up on the bed beside me. "Do you think Parker's falling for me as hard as I'm falling for him?"

Fuzzy looked at me and swished his tail against the bed. Little bursts of hope shot upward inside my heart, tiny firecrackers in the darkness.

You can't really assume the dog knows how Parker feels. I could always count on my cynical mind.

I mentally rolled my eyes. I trusted dogs more than some humans. They were pure of heart.

Chapter Twenty-Two

PARKER

"Oh, fuck!" My breath hissed through my teeth as I moved out of the way.

Hudson looked back from where he was ahead of me. "You okay?"

We were scheduled to fly out first thing tomorrow morning. We'd hiked a solid mile outside of the swath of the forest charred by the fire.

"Just a branch falling," I replied.

He glanced over his shoulder, cracking a grin. "Job hazard."

"About another mile," Graham called from up ahead.

We were all tired and more than ready to go home. For the first time since I'd been a hotshot firefighter, I had someone waiting for me at home. I couldn't wait to get back to see Luna. I figured she'd spoiled Fuzzy the entire time, and he'd probably want to stay with her forever.

The trees opened up along a rocky ledge, and we carefully picked our way across. The footing was rocky and easy to slip on here. We were almost in the clear when we heard a ragged shout. When we stopped, I glanced back to see Kincaid had slipped and fallen a good twenty feet below the trail.

We swung into action when he called up that it looked like he broke his ankle. It was handy to have a twenty-five-person crew all trained in wilderness first-responder emergency care. Within the hour, I'd rappelled down to Kincaid, and we'd gotten him back to safe ground. He was going to be fine. I had a run-in with a rock and sported a nasty gash on my shoulder. I knew I'd be fine, but I also knew I might need stitches.

Kincaid hobbled over with Hudson supporting him on one side. "Sorry about that, dude."

"Scars are badass," Hudson quipped with a quick glance over his shoulder.

I chuckled. "Minus the nuisance."

Hudson helped Kincaid ease down to sit against some backpacks.

"It doesn't even hurt at the moment. It's gonna sting when we clean it. I'm just glad you're okay," I said to Kincaid. "I knew that stretch of trail was a little dicey. Too much loose rock."

We made it back to camp with plenty of daylight

to spare, although it was approaching evening. Graham volunteered to clean up my gash. "He does the best butterfly bandaging," Wes called over.

Graham rolled his eyes and started going through the first aid supplies. "I don't even know if you need stitches, but we're gonna have to clean the hell out of this thing. Do you want some lidocaine on it before I pour the alcohol over?" he asked.

"They both sting," I retorted. "Just make it burn."

The following morning, Nate Fox picked us up to fly us back to Willow Brook. He was one of a number of pilots who flew hotshot firefighter crews in and out of Alaska's wilderness. He glanced over at me when I was lifting my pack with one arm. "Heard you got a nice little cut," he commented.

"Something like that." I winced when I shrugged.

Nate chuckled, taking my pack from me and loading it in the storage compartment on the bottom of the small plane. "You get to go on the first trip. Two more planes are headed this way. We prioritize anybody who might need medical treatment."

In short order, we were in the air, with about half the crew in this first flight with Nate. Graham had done an excellent job cleaning and closing up the gash on my arm. Yet, he insisted I still had to go to the hospital when we landed.

"Really?" I protested on the flight back.

Graham rolled his head to the side where he sat across the narrow aisle from me. "Yes. You don't need to go to the ER. We'll go to the walk-in clinic there. It's protocol. We need to make sure it won't get infected. If they recommend stitches, you're gonna have to accept it."

"I don't think I need anything," I grumbled.

Graham shrugged. "Enjoy the view on the way home," he teased.

Travel to and from work as a hotshot firefighter in Alaska meant absolutely stunning views. We left the fire completely contained with another hotshot crew arriving from Fairbanks to do more preventative work and make sure the fire remained fully contained.

The landscape of the interior part of Alaska, which was mountainous and thick with trees, shifted to taller mountains closer to the coast with Denali standing tall as the centerpiece.

"Are we landing in Willow Brook?" I asked.

Graham glanced over, nodding. "Yeah. One of the planes is landing in Anchorage behind us because they have a split group, but I made sure we're going straight home." Graham waggled his brows.

When the plane landed in Willow Brook, I experienced something new—a sense of joy and anticipation, knowing I would be seeing Luna soon. We all piled off of the plane, and I watched as Graham jogged across from where the plane landed to sweep Madison and their young son into a hug.

I wasn't expecting to see Luna, so I was surprised when I heard someone call my name. I thought my ears were tricking me when I lifted my head to glance around, but my heart was already kicking hard against my ribs. Luna was here. When I saw her walking over with Fuzzy bounding at her side on a leash, emotion rushed through me so fast, my lungs seized for a moment.

"Hey!" she called.

Seconds later, I was wrapping her in my arms and holding on tight. I ignored the sting of pain in my shoulder as I held her close and breathed her in. When I stepped back, her eyes were sparkling, and a gust of wind blew her curls wild while Fuzzy circled my legs rapidly.

"I missed you," she said.

Chapter Twenty-Three

LUNA

Parker stared at me for a long moment, and I worried I shouldn't have said anything. He gave his head a little shake, palming my cheek as he dropped his forehead against mine. "I missed you too."

His words shaped over my lips, and the raspy sound of his voice sent my belly swooping before he gave me a lingering kiss. We broke apart when someone called Parker's name.

I glanced over to see Nate Fox approaching with Parker's gear bag. I recognized it from the day he'd packed it up when he was leaving. "Hey, Luna," Nate said as he stopped beside us, dropping the heavy bag on the ground.

"Hey, Nate, did you fly them back?"

"I sure did." He nudged his chin toward Parker.

"Graham told me to tell you to make sure to take him to the walk-in clinic at the hospital."

"Huh?" was all I could manage.

Graham stopped beside us. "I actually have to go with you."

"What the hell for?" Parker muttered.

Graham glanced toward me as worry sliced through me. "He injured his shoulder on the rocks. I'm going over with Kincaid as well. Before you get too worried, Parker is fine. Everybody's fine, but it's protocol. Kincaid probably needs to get his ankle set, or at least braced. Parker needs clearance that there's no infection, and he may or may not need stitches."

Graham was way too calm for this. "Stitches?!" I exclaimed.

Madison approached, stopping at my side. "Life with firefighters. It sounds like everyone's gonna be fine," she said encouragingly. "Why don't you let Graham take them and you and I can go get coffee?"

When I looked at her, she slid her hand through my elbow and squeezed. "I have to go with him," I insisted.

When I met Parker's gaze, I wasn't sure what he wanted. "Do you want me to go with you, or do you want me to wait with Madison at the café?"

Fuzzy continued to circle his legs until Parker knelt down to pet him thoroughly. "Graham has to go with me," he said with a put-upon sigh as he straightened again. "Why don't you meet us there in about a half hour? I promise you I'm fine."

"I'm going with you," I insisted.

Parker's lips curled in a slow smile. "Okay."

A short drive later, we were in the waiting area at the walk-in care clinic at the hospital. I'd left Fuzzy in the car with a chew toy and the windows cracked open after a brief bathroom break for him. Holly usually worked in the ER, but she came over to check in. Madison had come with me to keep me company after calling Graham's older daughter to pick up their son.

"I've already seen Parker. He's fine," Holly assured me.

"Why aren't you back there with him?" I demanded.

Holly didn't even react to my demanding tone. "Because they don't need me. He doesn't even need stitches. They're doing a deep clean and putting a fresh bandage on."

I let out an impatient sigh. "Is it bad?"

Holly shook her head. "He'll have a nice scar from meeting with a sharp rock. There are plenty of options in the wilderness of Alaska for that. He's good." She tipped her head to the side, her assessing gaze studying me for a beat. "It's official."

"Agreed," Madison said, pressing her lips together to keep from smiling.

"What's official?" I was legitimately confused.

"You're in love," Holly said, all matter of fact.

Alarm jolted my heart. "I don't think I'm in love. I mean," I paused, considering my feelings for a minute before reality all but punched me in the chest. "Oh, my God." I dropped my face into my hands and let out a sigh. When I lifted my head again and my hands fell to my lap, they were both waiting with knowing smiles on their faces. "Is this love? When I'm in a panic and I'm afraid Parker might die from a cut?"

"Would you be panicking this much about a friend? Holly has clearly told you he's going to be fine, so there's no need to panic," Madison pointed out calmly.

My breath puffed my cheeks as I let it out. "Oh, my God," I repeated. "I'm not ready to say that out loud."

"Understood," Holly said, her lips twitching.

"Pretty sure Parker's in love with you too," Madison said hopefully. "I saw the way he looked at you. He wasn't expecting you to show up at the airport." She waggled her brows. "And he was really happy to see you.

"Oh, my God."

———

I insisted on bringing Parker back to my place. "I have food and everything. Fuzzy loves it there."

Parker's gaze slid toward me in the car. All the while, Fuzzy's tail was squishing back and forth on the seat behind him, and his chin was resting on Parker's shoulder. He was so happy Parker was home.

"You don't have to baby me," Parker said with a sigh. "I assure you I'm fine. I didn't even need stitches."

"I know." My heart twisted just thinking that he might've needed stitches. "We can get takeout for dinner, and I can make something for dessert and—"

Parker reached across the console between us, resting his palm on my knee and giving me a reassuring squeeze. "I'm home, Luna." He cleared his throat. "I'm really glad you came to get me."

My heart felt like it was tumbling down a hill, the beat racing at a breakneck pace. My emotions were so intense, it felt as if they were pressing against my skin.

When we got back to my house, a giddy sense of joy was spinning inside. I was just so plain happy to have Parker home. Fuzzy had no qualms about containing his happiness. He spun in circles and yipped in excitement when we let him out of the car. Parker played fetch with him for a few minutes. I watched from the porch, realizing I could get used to this.

This feeling of being at my little house with a happy dog and Parker, it felt like home. This moment in time held everything I'd craved in those years when my parents were crisscrossing Alaska and the country. Stability, a place to call my own, and a person there with me for all of it.

Fuzzy brought back the ball one last time, and Parker turned to approach the porch where I stood halfway up the steps. Emotion rushed up, crashing through me while tears stung my eyes.

Parker stopped in front of me at the base of the stairs, while Fuzzy circled my legs. I buried a hand in his fur, stroking through it as Fuzzy leaned against my legs.

Parker's eyes were level with mine where he stood one step below me. "Are you okay?" he asked, a line appearing between his brows, a little furrow of worry, as concern chased through his gaze.

I felt silly, overcome with emotion to have him home and feeling all of these mundane, domestic thoughts. "I'm good, I promise. Really good."

His gaze softened as he took a step closer. He caught my free hand with his and palmed my cheek with the other, leaning close to brush a kiss over my lips. "I'm really glad to be home, Luna," he murmured over my lips when he lifted his head.

My belly filled with butterflies, tingles radiating everywhere. "I'm really glad you're here," I whispered.

Fuzzy shimmied between our legs, and we glanced down together. The sound of Parker's chuckle spun into the sensations in my body. It felt like the windows to my heart had been thrown wide open, and his presence was filling me with sunshine and light and happiness.

Just then, Parker's stomach growled. A chuckle rustled in his throat. "I guess I don't have to tell you I'm hungry."

A little while later, Fuzzy was happily asleep in the living room. I'd made a quick dinner for Parker, one of my staples from our years on the road, a simple meal of pasta with whatever veggies I had on hand, a dash of red peppers with feta and olive oil. It was tasty, filling, and yummy.

When he told me he'd missed my donuts, I used the dough I already had and made him some on the spot. I glanced at the timer on the stove as I tucked away the last dish in the dishwasher. "Three minutes," I tossed over my shoulder.

"Luna, you didn't have to do all this."

"You've been away, and you needed a shower." I grinned over at him as I dried my hands on a dish towel. "You were filthy," I pointed out.

He threw his head back with a laugh. "I was. Hazards of the job. Normally, we would land and go back to the station, and I would shower there, but you met me at the airport."

Airports in small Alaskan towns were officially airports, but nothing like an airport in a big area. There was a small runway as they mostly serviced the array of small single-engine and two-engine planes that dotted the skies of Alaska on a daily basis. Even in isolated rural areas, there were small landing strips for planes to land. Some of the Alaskan native villages that served as hubs for the other areas had over one hundred planes a day pass through. With Alaska's vast geography, the small planes were even called air taxis and functioned as such.

"How's your shoulder?" I asked.

Parker leaned back in his chair, rolling said shoulder lightly. "It's fine. A little sore, but it's just a cut."

Pressing my lips together, I narrowed my eyes. "You make it seem like it's the equivalent of a paper cut. Graham wouldn't have insisted you get cleared at the urgent care walk-in if he didn't think it was important."

Parker let out a sigh. "It's just deep enough that there could've been a risk of infection. The clinic confirmed I'm good to go."

I tossed the dish towel on the counter and walked across the kitchen, leaning down to press a kiss on his cheek. He slid his arm around my waist and brought his mouth to mine. A moment later, my knees were weak after he laid a tongue-tangling kiss on me. We broke apart when the oven buzzer went off.

My breath was coming in heaves, and I could barely stand. "I have to take those out," I rasped.

His palm smoothed over my hip before he gave my bottom a squeeze. "Hurry and then come right back."

On wobbly knees, I crossed the kitchen to take the donuts out of the oven and put them on top. Seconds later, I was standing before him again, and he tugged me onto his lap. I straddled him as our kisses melted from one into the next. My hips rocked over the hard ridge of his arousal, and I could feel the slick moisture in my core. I was restless, reckless, and desperate for him. I whimpered when he blazed a trail of wet kisses down my neck, his teeth grazing lightly.

He unbuttoned my blouse, swiftly snapping open the clasp between my breasts. He cupped them, his thumbs teasing over my aching nipples just before his mouth closed over one. He gave a hard suck, and my hands speared his hair as I let out a sharp cry.

"I need you." His voice was husky and commanding at once.

We stared at each other, breath heaving, and all I knew was I needed him. The next few moments were a messy scramble. Shimmying off his lap, I kicked my jeans off.

We couldn't stop touching each other as we fumbled. I wanted to feel his skin, and I slid my hand up under his shirt, savoring the heat emanating from him. He tugged his shirt up over his head. We were in too much of a rush. He stumbled and almost fell when I swiftly unbuttoned his jeans to slide my hand in and curl it around his hot, velvety length. He almost knocked the chair over, tugging me close as he sat down.

Just when I was about to straddle him and sink down over his length, he stopped me with his palm gripping my hip tightly. "We need a condom," he bit out.

"I'm on birth control," I whispered.

When I first moved away from my parents, my grandmother had a direct, practical conversation with me about it because she wasn't sure my mom had. For all of my mom's faults, she had talked with me about it, but routine medical appointments weren't part of my life until I moved away. My grandmother made sure I found a good doctor, and I'd started birth control to keep my cycle regular.

Parker held my gaze for several long seconds. "Are you sure? Because I can wear a condom."

"Am I sure that I'm on birth control?" My cheeks burned.

"I know you know that. I just want to make sure it's okay if I don't wear a condom. I promise you we're all good health-wise for me."

"I know," I whispered, pausing to suck in a breath. "Please. I want to feel you inside me. Completely." I didn't even know how to put into words how much I wanted to feel that.

His eyes burned into mine as he tugged me back

over his lap. I felt the press of his thick crown notching at my slippery entrance. One of his hands slid up my back to land between my shoulder blades as the other gripped my hip. Impatient and restless, I sank down swiftly, crying out in relief and pleasure at the feel of him filling me.

I felt the press of his fingers into my hip. He seated himself fully inside of me, levering me forward with his palm in the center of my back. My heartbeat echoed through me. He leaned closer, whispering, "Luna."

I dragged my eyes open. "I missed you," he rasped, the words brushing over my lips.

"I missed you too." Staring into his eyes, a rushing sensation built inside of me.

I didn't expect myself to say what I said next, but it just slipped out. As if the emotion itself was rushing through me and had to be spoken aloud. "I love you, Parker." The moment the words were whispered, a jolt of anxiety and fear struck me. I almost panicked, but he never looked away.

I felt the brush of his thumb down along the edge of one of my shoulder blades as his gaze held mine. "I love you, Luna," he whispered back to me, the *you* said with a definitive edge to it.

He rocked his hips, nudging deeper into me. I rose up, sinking down over him. That rushing feeling sped faster and faster as we rocked together. The friction from where we were joined teased my climax to its edge until he reached between us and gave me the exact pressure I needed. I cried out, his name a ragged gasp as the pleasure radiated through me like rays of light splitting me apart as he held me close. I felt him thrust upward once more, and then he was shuddering along with me, his fingers clenching where he held me. I collapsed against him as he held me close. Through all of this, my sense of coming home was complete.

Chapter Twenty-Four

PARKER

A week later

I walked out of the workout area at the fire station and aimed for the showers. I was getting dressed a few minutes later when Hudson came walking in. He plunked down on the bench across from me.

"How's that shoulder?" he asked.

I rolled it and shrugged. "Pretty good, not much soreness left."

Hudson nodded, tipping his head to the side as he studied me when I sat down to put on my shoes. When he didn't say anything else, I glanced up to see him looking at his phone with a small smile. "Text from Stella?" I asked.

Hudson's smile stretched wide as he nodded.

"Awesome." I chuckled. "Dude, you are seriously whipped."

He shrugged unabashedly. "I am. I love it too."

Tossing my towel into the laundry bin against the wall, I shook my head. "Who knew you'd fall that hard?" I teased.

"How's Luna?" My friend's brows hitched up as he held my gaze.

"I'm sure you've seen her at the coffee shop," I hedged.

Hudson eyed me. "Ah, so that's how you're gonna try to play it."

I pressed my tongue into my cheek, fighting a smile. Hudson knew me well. Although we'd only reconnected as friends over the last year, the time we spent together in detention during high school had bonded us deeply. "I'm not playing, she means a lot, and—" I paused, a sneaky sense of uncertainty slithering through me. I knew how I felt about Luna, but it had taken me by surprise. "All joking aside, I don't really know what to do," I said bluntly.

Hudson's gaze sobered instantly. "What do you mean?"

I let out a heavy sigh, resting my elbows on my knees and tunneling my hands through my hair. A few seconds ticked by before I straightened and dropped my hands. "You know, I don't have a lot of faith in stability. I always figured I would just take care of myself and that would be pretty fucking good in this life." Hudson and I shared similar histories and not just because we both had flaky dads who zigzagged in and out of trouble. My dad was doing well now. He was sober and happily in love with Stella's mom, the whole one-big-happy-family deal come true.

Bless my dad's flaky heart. I appreciated everything he did, but the little boy I'd been at the time my mom had dropped me off had been in shock. My dad had been a stranger to me at first. Every time I thought about my mom and what it took for her to just dump me like that, I experienced a mix of abandonment, confusion, and burning anger.

Hudson leaned forward, his concerned gaze skating over my face. "I do know, but it doesn't have to stay that way. It's worth giving someone a chance." He waved one hand dismissively. "Don't think I'm being all mushy. I'm not one of those people who thinks you have to be partnered up and do the happy family dance. You know, like Beck," he said dryly.

A low laugh rustled in my throat. Beck meant well, but he was a true believer in love and all that. "If the way you feel about Luna is anything like the way I feel about Stella, it's worth it. I know what happened with your mom sucked, believe me, I get it. But not everyone's like that. Your dad sure isn't. That man stepped up for you. He's rock solid."

"I know." My heart felt scraped raw. These were

old wounds. I'd lived with the motto it was best to let old pain stay buried. This was not something I wanted to open up.

"Maybe you should go see a therapist, you know the one, the one Leo and Casey see?" my friend suggested.

"Are you serious?" I sputtered.

As if on cue, Leo came walking into the locker room. "What's your therapist's name?" Hudson asked.

Leo sat down on the bench across from me. "Delaney. She's awesome. Why do you ask?"

"I was just telling Parker maybe he should go see her."

Leo's gaze shifted to me. "I say go for it. I don't even know what this is about, but I promise Delaney can help you figure it out."

"Oh, my God," I muttered.

"Hey, therapy isn't for cowards," Leo replied, looking affronted by my reaction.

I shook my head with a sigh. "That's not it. I've been to therapy, back in high school. I got nothing against it, but..." I ran out of words.

"I think he's in love with Luna and he's freaking out," Hudson chimed in.

"Dude, we don't have to have a group conversation about this," I muttered.

"Luna is nice, you clearly love her, and those

donuts—" Leo whistled, pressing his fingertips together in the chef's kiss gesture. "Fucking amazing."

"I agree. They are. No argument there," I replied.

Leo arched a brow as he studied me. "Look, it's not my business, but it seems like you and Luna are pretty good together. I definitely understand not being sure about things like that, but I'm also on team love-makes-the-world-a-better-place."

I snorted. "Dude you're still in the honeymoon phase with Casey."

"Yep, it's fucking amazing. She's the best thing that ever happened to me," he said flatly. His expression went from teasing to dead serious in a flash. "I'll text you Delaney's number. I don't think Casey and I will ever stop seeing her. We only go like," he wiggled his hand back and forth, "once a month or so now, but it's super helpful. Not to mention, I'm basically an instant soup dad, and it's great to have someone to check in with about that."

Chapter Twenty-Five

PARKER

While I was busy wondering whether or not to call Delaney, things kept rolling along with Luna. Maybe I wasn't sure how to handle my feelings for her, but I couldn't stay away. I was walking into the station a few days later when Maisie called my name from the front. When I walked out there, she was at her desk, and an unfamiliar woman was standing at the counter.

Maisie smiled over at me. "Hi Parker, this woman is here to see you."

Although my brain didn't quite recognize her, my heart knew this person was my mother. A sense of sheer panic slammed into me. I kept it together and just stood there by the door into the back hallway. "What can I do for you?" I hated that my voice sounded hoarse.

"Parker, do you remember me?"

I shrugged. "Maybe, maybe not."

Maisie appeared to sense my distress or sheer discombobulation. Sometimes it felt like everything in the world was a step in a path to a moment. In this case, a reckoning. Little boy me had wanted for so long for my mom to come back. Here she was now, and I wanted to vomit and to scream and shout. Instead, I stood there. Static filled my brain. It was a miracle I didn't fall because it also felt as if someone had tripped me.

"I'm your mom," my mother said.

I stared at her. "Uh-huh." I didn't know what she expected, but it seemed like maybe she thought I'd give her a big ol' hug.

Maisie rounded the corner and literally stood in front of me when my mom turned and began to approach me. I could sense Maisie's protectiveness. She took care of all of us here at the station. As the main dispatcher, she was, both literally and metaphorically, the switchboard through which all communication flowed. In this moment, I could feel a deeper level of protectiveness. I knew if I needed her to, Maisie would physically walk my mom out of the station.

Somehow, her sense of protectiveness settled me and balanced me. I still felt a little staticky inside, and my heart felt hollow, but I kept my eyes on my mother and calmly said, "I'm not sure what you expected after all this time, but I don't really need you now."

My mother stared at me, her eyes going a little wide and tears shimmering there. Maybe that should've hurt, and I should've felt something more, but I just didn't. I didn't owe her anything. I couldn't say anything more and turned and walked to the back. I distantly heard Maisie saying, "You can't go back there. That's for staff only." Her tone was clear and determined as if she was disciplining a child.

I kept it together long enough to go through the back to grab my jacket and walk out to my truck in the back parking lot. I climbed in and pulled up Leo's text, immediately leaving a message for the therapist.

When Luna texted me later, for the first night since I'd gotten back from the fire, I didn't go over there. I told her I didn't feel good, but I didn't tell her why. Of course, to make matters more complicated, Fuzzy was staying at her place. He adored Luna. I knew he was technically my dog, and he adored me too, but her place was better. She had more space, and she could let him run loose there.

Chapter Twenty-Six

LUNA

"What do you think?" Janet asked.

"Are you really serious about this?" I looked from Janet to my grandmother uncertainly.

Janet reached across the table, curling her weathered hands around both of mine and squeezing. "Absolutely." She released my hands and leaned back in her chair. "I've already talked to my accountant and my attorney. It's all set up. You just need to decide if this is what you want. You'll still be able to bake your donuts, but taking on the café is, well, something else. That's why I structured this the way I did. I'll maintain ownership for five years. I'll hire you as a manager. After three years, I'll start tapering off my time there. I want to be able to work as long as I can, but I know I can't work full-time forever. With this plan, if something changes, like my health or something, then you can just slide right in."

I took a quick breath. "I absolutely want this. I just can't believe it."

Janet smiled warmly. "I've been worrying on what to do with my business for years. You know your grandma is one of my best friends. Since you were a little girl, I've considered you an honorary grand-daughter and had you in mind for this. Then you moved away, so I wasn't sure what to do until you came back."

"The RV life upended so many things," I said dryly.

"Something like that," Janet replied with a shrug.

"I think you should do it, Luna," my grand-mother chimed in. "You'll love it. It's a great fit for you. The business is stable enough that you'll have staff and you can keep baking. You have a place to live, and you'll have the café." My grandmother let out a little happy sound. "You'll be settled, which I know is what you always wanted."

I glanced between them. "I love you both so much!" I exclaimed.

Stella beamed at me. "I love this for you!" She was handling the legal paperwork for Janet's plan for the cafe.

"I love it too," I said. "I'm nervous. A little."

Stella tipped her head to the side, her gaze studying me quietly. "Okay, hear me out. You're already making the best donuts in the universe." She gestured with her hand in a big circle in the air. "You already help out front. You're just gonna step in and be in charge." She nodded vigorously in emphasis.

"I know, but Janet is the center of Firehouse Café. Honestly, she's the center of Willow Brook." I let out a quick sigh. "How will it be when I'm the owner? What if everybody just stops coming?"

Stella sat back in her chair, her gaze softening. "Okay, I understand. I'm newer to town than you. Janet might be the glue that holds so many people together." She pressed her palm to her chest. "She's always wonderful, but she also makes killer coffee and has amazing food. I don't think the business would be as solid as it is if she hadn't made strategic choices, no matter how nice she is. You're not planning any changes, except even better baked goods. They run out of donuts literally every day because you can't bake them fast enough."

A flush of pride rose inside, and I felt my lips curling into a smile. "Okay. It's just I kind of can't believe it."

"Well, you'd better believe it," she replied with a grin.

"What if people think I'm trying to take it from Janet?"

"Oh, my God! You worry more than me. Nobody will think that. Janet is one-hundred percent of sound mind. She can't work forever, so she's making plans. Take a deep breath and let yourself enjoy this moment. You know what I think?"

"Um, all of that?" I returned.

"Well, yes, and this calls for a girls' night. Maybe not cards because we just did that last week, but I'm gonna message our group chat. Let's go to the winery for dinner and drinks. We need to celebrate you and your future." Her thumbs were already tapping away on her phone screen.

Seconds later, my phone vibrated on the table with her text. Replies came in fast. She set her phone on the table and tidied up the papers, tucking them into a file folder. "Speaking of your future, how are things with Parker?"

Before I even opened my mouth, my expression must've given me away. My heart felt a little bruised. I didn't know why, but it seemed as if Parker was vaguely avoiding me. I still had Fuzzy, which was fine because I loved that dog to pieces, but something felt out of whack.

I quickly filled her in, ending with, "And, I don't know!" I lifted my hands and let them fall. "I feel so stupid."

"Don't. You haven't done anything wrong," Stella assured me.

"I told him I loved him, and now this."

"Did he say it back?" she asked, adding, "I'm just trying to figure out if he panicked."

I nodded, blinking and doing my best not to cry.

"Well, it's a good thing we're having dinner tonight. Maisie already said she'll be there. If anybody knows what might be going on with Parker, she'll find out if she doesn't already know."

Chapter Twenty-Seven

LUNA

That evening, a waitress seated our group in a room off the side of the main dining area at Fireweed Winery & Restaurant. "People reserve these for events and such, but we don't have any scheduled tonight. It's a little quieter in here. My name is Tori." She tapped the little name tag on her chest. "Don't hesitate to yell if you need something," she teased.

Farrah smiled up at her. "We won't yell. That would be rude."

"It would be funny." Tori waggled her brows. "For now, figure out your drink orders, and I'll be back in a flash."

Along with Stella and me, Farrah, Tiffany, Josie, Casey, Tish, Maisie, Madison, Amelia, and Jasmine were here. I looked around the table. "This is amazing."

"What's amazing?" Jasmine asked from my side. Along with many of the women I'd reconnected with, Jasmine had gone to the same elementary school as me. She'd been a few grades ahead of me. I'd always liked her, even though we hadn't been that close growing up. What had felt like a chasm in age when we were little now didn't feel like much of anything.

I smiled at her. "Just being here, being in Willow Brook, having friends," I said softly.

Jasmine curled her arm around my shoulders and squeezed. "It's good to have you back home."

Stella insisted we all toast to celebrate my news. Rumor had it, Janet had already started talking about it at the café.

"I'm so happy for you, but also for Janet. She can start to slow down," Maisie offered.

Stella waggled her brows. "See," she teased.

"See what?" Tiffany prompted.

"Luna was worried that somehow people would be upset about this," Stella explained.

A collection of voices chimed in to assure me Janet couldn't do it forever, and they were just happy that I would be taking over. "Your donuts are amazing, so the baked goods and food will get even better," Maisie said. "Firehouse Café has great food, but your donuts are greater than great."

"Greater than great, for sure," Amelia said, lifting her glass in another small toast.

Once we had a selection of appetizers to choose from, Stella nudged Maisie, who was sitting beside her. "What's the scoop? Do you have any gossip on Parker? Completely serious question."

Maisie glanced at me first as she nodded. "He's really stressed out."

Worry slid through me. "What's going on?" Amelia asked.

Stella jumped in, "He's quietly avoiding Luna, and she doesn't know what's going on."

Maisie sighed. "Well, his mom came into the station. The mom who dumped him with his father when he was just a little boy. He literally hasn't seen or heard from her since then." Maisie shook her head. "She's come in like twice since the first time, and I haven't even told him. Because he told me he didn't want to see her. I asked Beck and Hudson to let me know if Parker changes his mind. I feel protective of him. I'm a mom, so I can't imagine what she did. I understand that people go through things and that life happens, and so on. I'm sure we don't have the whole story, but he was six, and he hasn't seen her since. She seemed to think he'd be ecstatic to see her and now she's sad about it." Maisie shook her head.

"I asked Hudson when I got home." Stella caught my eye. "He doesn't have many details other than that Parker's mom showed up at the station. Well, that, and Parker seems like he's been in a bad mood for the last three days straight. Hudson told me that Leo suggested he talk to that therapist. I sure hope he did."

I felt near frantic inside. I wanted to call Parker right away, but he wasn't talking to me about this. "I don't know what to do. Should I call him? Should I get pushy? This is my first serious relationship. Honestly, it's my first relationship at all."

Jasmine summed up the general consensus. "I might not know Parker as well as Stella, Hudson, and you, obviously, but I don't think this is the kind of thing you push about. Let him know you're there if he wants to talk. That's pretty heavy stuff."

Tiffany chimed in, "Take it from someone else who had a really screwed up mom, give him space. Having his mom show up like that would be a mind-fuck," she said flatly. Her lips turned down as she grimaced.

I let out a breath, the air blowing out in a puff. "I'll text him and let him know I'm here if he wants to talk."

After the heaviness of that conversation, my friends went out of their way to keep the conversation funny and light. There were hugs all around when we left. As I drove home, I was beyond grateful to feel like I had my people. Ever since my parents had hopped in that RV and taken me along with them, I'd felt lonely.

Chapter Twenty-Eight

LUNA

Me: it seems like you've been busy. I totally understand! Just letting you know I'm here if you need anything. Also, do you want me to bring Fuzzy back?

I re-read the text I'd sent Parker this morning, maybe for the hundredth time. I'd agonized over the wording. I didn't want to seem like I'd been gossiping about him, but I also wanted him to know I was there. I also didn't want to seem desperate, even though I was feeling completely desperate. I'd told him I loved him and now he was ignoring me.

Fuzzy's fluffy tail swished on the floor where he sat by the kitchen table.

"Hey, buddy." I scratched the back of his neck, and he let out this happy growly sound he made whenever I did that.

I'd sent that text a solid hour ago and had no reply yet. A sigh slipped out.

"Whatever," I muttered, as I stared down at my phone screen that had gone dark.

Restless, I looked up from the table and glanced at my watch. "I'll go to work," I said to Fuzzy.

Hours ago, I'd made the morning batch of donuts. I could make more because we always ran out.

I stared at myself in the mirror a few minutes later, my curls damp around my shoulders. "This is what he's reduced you to," I said to my reflection in the mirror. "Talking to yourself in the mirror. In the third person. Ugh!"

I spun away from my reflection and yanked the hairdryer out of a drawer, cursing my curls because I needed to use the diffuser to keep them from going wild when I dried them. It felt like forever. After I had dried my hair, I dressed and rushed out into the crisp autumn morning.

Fuzzy was a great little car companion. While Fuzzy couldn't go into the kitchen with me, because of kitchen cleanliness regulations, Jasmine always let him spend time with her in her pottery studio behind the cafe.

"Okay, Fuzzy," I said, as I fished out one of his favorite rolled-up rawhide chews. He would work on these for hours if he wasn't asleep. "You be a good boy."

Jasmine was working and waved at me as she looked up. When I walked into the kitchen at Firehouse Café, I experienced a little spurt of happiness and a break from dwelling on Parker. The sounds of a busy morning filtered back from the front. I took a breath, savoring the scents of coffee and food. I realized this place would become mine. I almost burst into tears at the idea of it.

A little while later, I was busy at work, starting the process of shaping the donuts to bake. Just when I had talked myself into being at peace with the fact that it seemed like Parker and I might not be what I hoped, Casey came walking in the back with a worried look on her face.

"What's up?" I asked, not even considering myself in the equation of her worry.

"Your parents are here."

"Huh?"

"Your parents, you know the RV parents," she explained, as if I had another set of parents.

"Are you serious?"

Casey's ponytail bounced with her nod. "Uh-huh, and they're filming, and there are some tourists out there who know who they are. They're all excited. They are hoping you're going to come out front. I wanted to lie and say you weren't even here, but they saw your car." Casey twisted her hands together.

"It's fine, Casey. You aren't in charge of lying to my parents. I can handle them." I quickly finished shaping the donuts and slid the proofing trays into the case.

Although I had plenty of messy emotions around my parents and our years in the RV, I hadn't ghosted them. We checked in by phone and texted, but I should've known they would do a surprise stop in Willow Brook. That was how they handled things when they didn't want me to have a say in the situation.

"Do you want me to tell them they can't film?" she asked.

I shook my head. "It's fine, Casey. Honestly, I'd rather them film here in public, where they have to try to behave themselves, than for them to do something privately and set it all up. That's the more obnoxious option."

I hated how my stomach twisted with dread and my old annoying friend, anxiety, began spinning in my chest. I dusted my hands on my apron before washing them. Just before I started to walk into the front, I glanced toward Casey who was at my side. "Please interrupt if something gets weird."

"You got it! Josie's here too."

I swallowed and followed her out front. My parents were standing off to the side at the register, filming and chatting with some people who appeared to know who they were.

"There she is!" My mom stretched her arms wide as I rounded the counter. She enveloped me in a hug, all the while my dad was filming away and narrating, complete with referring to me as "the prodigal daughter."

"What do you think, sweetie?" my mom asked as she stepped back. "How about a few days on the road with us?"

The knots in my stomach twisted even tighter. "I can't, Mom," I said, trying to keep my expression neutral. "I'm working."

One of the customers interjected, "We loved it when you were on the channel. We miss you, Jane! And wow, look at those curls. Did you get a perm?"

I wanted to disappear into the floor. I hated this. I forgot how much I hated it. Just then, as if it couldn't get any worse, Parker came walking in. His eyes landed on me, and I smiled tightly at him.

Josie came to my rescue, zooming around the counter. "We really need you in the back right now."

"Okay!" I chirped. I gave my mom and dad quick hugs. "I'll text you this afternoon. Are you just driving through?"

"We'll be here for a few days," my dad replied.

"Ohmygodohmygodohmygod," I breathed as soon as I got in the back. "Do not let them come back here." I lifted my eyes to Josie.

"Of course not! There's no way on God's green earth they are coming back here. What do you need?"

"Nothing." I bit back a sigh.

"What about Parker?" Josie asked.

"It's fine. There's nothing I can do."

Josie's concerned gaze studied me for a beat. "Give it time."

All I could do was shrug. I didn't have the emotional bandwidth for more.

When I left the kitchen, my parents were waiting for me in the parking lot in the back with their RV. My world was bunching up together, a traffic jam of stress and anxiety.

I decided to barrel through the situation with my parents. I smiled at them tightly. "I'm not traveling anywhere if that's what you were hoping. It's great to see you. Let's have dinner at Gram's tonight."

"Jane," my dad started.

Using that name cued me that he was filming. He still had a camera mounted on the side of the RV. I bit back a sigh. I didn't miss, not even a little, the ever-present feeling of being on camera.

"We really miss you, and we'd love to do a short trip together!" my mom interjected.

I shook my head sharply, clenching my teeth to contain the anger rising inside. "See you tonight." I tripped as I was hurrying over to my car. I belatedly glanced up to see Parker waiting beside it. My nerves tightened in my stomach.

"What is it, Parker?" I asked.

He looked torn, with lines of tension tightening

as his eyes coasted over my face. "Just wondering how you're doing."

I gaped at him. "What the fuck, Parker? Not great." With my parents showing up and stripping away my privacy, my tolerance for anything was gone. "Just dump me already," I said flatly. "Unless you're giving me Fuzzy, come get him. It feels really weird that I have him, and you're just ignoring me."

He looked completely stricken. I ignored the sharp sting of pain over my heart. "Now, I have to go."

I climbed into my car, just after hurrying over to fetch Fuzzy from Jasmine's studio. I just needed to get out of there.

Chapter Twenty-Nine

PARKER

"I don't even know what to do." I let out a heavy sigh as I rested my elbows on my knees, my head hanging forward.

I sat across from my therapist, Delaney. I was ignoring Luna, ignoring my mom, really, just ignoring my life.

"Okay, so let me get this straight. Your mom is here trying to make up with you, and Luna's parents are here too?" At my nod, Delaney added, "That's a lot."

Although this was only my third appointment with her, I felt completely comfortable with Delaney. I appreciated how she didn't hesitate to go directly into the challenging stuff. Straightening, I leaned back into the comfortable couch in her office. "It's definitely a lot."

"Let's deal with your mom first. Have you talked to her at all?"

"Like I explained, she came to see me at work, and we talked then. She's tried two more times. Maisie is basically holding her at bay. My mom doesn't have my number. Thank God she hasn't figured out where I live. Do I have to talk to her? What do you tell people whose parents do things like this?" I asked, honestly wondering.

"I tell them that there isn't one way in how you choose to handle this. I'll be honest, I don't believe in the idea of closure, if you will. When something really painful happens, there are ways to come to peace with it, but it's always a part of your life. You can't make anything disappear. You can learn how to deal with it. This is a messy situation. Whatever you choose to do now, you may change your mind later. And that's okay. Some people want to make a connection with the person who hurt them deeply and find a way to have it be peaceful. For others, there's too much pain. Your mom closed the door to you being in her life at one point. We don't know her reasons, but now she's trying to open it again. You were a little boy. What happened hurt you. In short, whatever you choose to do is entirely your choice. She wants something from you now. If I were her therapist, which I'm not and I won't be, I would let her know that this needs to be on your terms and that she would have to accept whatever your choice is. The stories we hear about on social media and in the news are usually the ones where families decide to reconnect and forgive each other and so on. Forgiveness doesn't mean you have to repair the relationship, and that's often forgotten. You can forgive someone and let go for your own peace, but it doesn't mean you have to foster a relationship with her. We don't know what's going on for her and her thought process, but that's not your responsibility. If you choose to have a conversation with her, I would definitely recommend writing down what you want to say. In emotionally loaded situations, that can be helpful."

I took a slow breath, considering my feelings and Delaney's feedback. "I'm not sure how I feel, but I do know I'm angry that she's here. I'm angry that she has these expectations."

Delaney's eyes were soft. "Being human is messy and relationships, in particular parent-child relationships, are complicated. In this case, your mother didn't fulfill a primary role for you. She abandoned you. That's what happened. Now, she wants to repair that rupture. What do you think you want?"

A corner of my heart was a throbbing ache. I couldn't have what I wanted. "I want my mom to have not done what she did, but since I can't have that, I guess I just want her not to do this." I chewed on the inside of my cheek, an old habit. I restlessly shook my wrists, almost trying to shake away the unsettled feeling inside. "I guess it would be different if I reached out. Maybe there's some good reason why she did what she did and maybe that's what she wants to tell me, but it still sucks."

Delaney nodded. "You were a little boy, and that hurt a lot. Knowing that you can't change the fact that she came to you now and that you definitely can't change the past, what do you think you want out of this?" She circled her hand in the air.

"I guess I want to hear her out, but I'm pretty sure I don't want to build a relationship with her, not right now." I twisted my lips to the side with a sigh. "It's annoying you can't tell me what to do." I rolled my eyes.

Delaney smiled sadly. "I can't tell you what to do here, although I understand wishing someone could."

"It helps that this doesn't have to feel final. Maybe you didn't tell me what to do, but you gave me that permission," I said.

"It really isn't final, not until she passes away," Delaney pointed out, her tone careful.

"And that's another thing," I said, shaking my head slightly. "What if she's coming out of the woods because she's sick and she's gonna die? For fuck's sake. What if? I have no idea."

"It is a possibility. There are plenty of people who come forward later in life, family members who try to reconnect when they're facing their own mortality. The experience of facing your mortality can be…" She paused for a moment. "Crystallizing, clarifying. It tends to bring things into focus. Even if that adds to your anger about it, which it does for many, it's not all bad. It can be one of those moments for some people where it's like, holy wow, I need to fix this, or at least say my peace. Because when it's too late, it's definitely too late. If you decide you want to talk to her and you want my support, I'm happy to help you have that conversation."

I snorted. "I know you would do that. Thank you."

"For…?"

"Fitting me in on short notice. For taking the time to talk things through. Honestly, I know not every therapist is for everybody, but I'm really glad I feel comfortable with you. I think I can handle the conversation with my mom on my own, and I'm gonna do it."

"You are?"

"Surprised?" I prompted.

"Not really. You've faced challenging conversations before, based on what little time I've had to learn. You seem ready to just go for it. Right now."

I shrugged. "I am. I need to banish these ghosts. I don't believe in closure either, so I'm damn glad we agree on that point. But even if I don't know if I want to build a relationship with my mom, I do want to have the conversation."

"Okay." Delaney's gaze was considering. "And, what about Luna?"

———

Damn if Delaney's question about Luna didn't sting. The pain around my mom in my heart was old and achy, while my feelings around Luna were sharp. Although my mom's reappearance in my life had kicked up a storm of doubts, the pain around Luna was different.

I didn't know what the fuck to do. I was terrified that I might do to Luna what my mom had done to me. In short, when it mattered, just bolt. What if I couldn't face the hard stuff? I was starting to realize it wasn't just my own fear of abandonment but what it represented. I was terrified that if I wasn't enough for Luna, that she would leave me in the dust. Just like my mom.

The little boy inside of me never stopped wondering if I'd been worthy enough if my mom wouldn't have stayed. She wouldn't have dropped me off. Even if there was some reasonable explanation for why she did that, why didn't she reach out sooner?

Despite so much internal confusion around Luna, the clarity I'd achieved around my mom held. I called her after I left my appointment.

"Parker!" my mom exclaimed.

Hearing her voice was disorienting. It was like a stored recording somewhere in my brain.

"Here's the deal," I jumped in. "I am *not* ready to have a relationship with you. I have no idea if I ever will. You forfeited the right to ask for one when you dumped me at my dad's and never reached out again until now. For what it's worth, Dad stepped up to the plate and I love him. I just want to know why."

My mother was quiet for a long moment before I heard the sound of her sigh filtering through the call. "Is it possible for us to have this conversation face-to-face?"

"Not right now." I didn't know what it was about Delaney's feedback, but I felt a sense of clarity I had never experienced around this.

"Okay. Do you remember the man I was dating at the time?" my mom asked.

I had vague memories of a man. "Not much. I remember I didn't like him. That's it."

"Well, there's no easy way for me to explain this, but I was young, and I didn't have good judgment in men. And Dan gave me an ultimatum. He told me that he didn't wanna deal with a kid, and I was afraid to be alone. I was also afraid of him because he was abusive, so I decided to take you to your dad even though your dad didn't know you existed then. I knew he was your father. I knew maybe he wasn't the greatest guy, but he was safe. Please tell me I was right about that."

I sat there, taking in her explanation. "You were right about that. He's always been safe and a good dad."

She let out another sigh, this one heavy and loud. "Thank God." She cleared her throat and continued. "So, uh, that's it. It took me almost twelve years to get away from Dan. By that point, I was embarrassed to reach out. I know that isn't a good excuse, but that's what happened. I know I hurt you, but I promise it was better for you to be with your dad. I did not have my life together. I loved you, but I didn't have it in me to do the right thing. I was worried that I couldn't keep you safe."

"It definitely wasn't the right thing," I said.

"I'm sorry." I could've sworn she sniffled a little, but I didn't have it in me to feel badly for her, not right now.

"Does it help to understand what happened?" she asked, her voice small.

"I don't really understand," I said honestly. "If Dan didn't want a kid, why didn't you just leave then?"

"I didn't know how. I know that's not a good answer, but it's the honest answer."

I took in a slow breath. "I'm not saying this to make you feel bad, but it really fucked me up. I'm okay, but it was really a mess for me."

"I'm more sorry than I can ever really express."

Silence echoed through the call. I wasn't sure

what else to say. At this moment, I knew I needed time. "I appreciate that you want to connect now, but I need time. I'm not sure when I'll want to reach out again, or if I will. I'm glad you told me the truth, or at least your version of it. I hope you can respect that I need time."

The quiet felt loud, almost reverberating with pain, before she whispered, "Okay. My phone number won't change. If something happens and you need to reach out, just call me. I'll be here whenever you're ready. Maybe it doesn't feel like it, but I love you, and I did love you."

"Okay," was all I could offer in response to that.

After I ended the call, I sat in my truck. I did a mental body scan. I felt a little hollow, but okay. I sensed there might become a time when I would reach back out, but it would have to wait until I felt ready. While I was sitting there, I abruptly decided I needed to go see Luna. I needed to explain. I tapped out a quick text.

Me: *I hope it's okay if I stop by. On the way.*

Chapter Thirty

PARKER

When I rolled to a stop in front of Luna's place, there was a big RV parked off to the side. Fuck. Her parents. I mentally buckled up and climbed out of my truck. When I knocked on the door and Luna answered, the stress on her face hurt me viscerally. Her features were tight with her eyes pinched at the corners and her mouth a tense straight line.

"Hey." Even her voice sounded strained.

My girl who liked to do tarot cards, who my dog adored, and who I'd been ignoring because I was a chickenshit, felt bruised. I wanted to chase her parents away.

We stared at each other for a long moment, and I sensed she didn't know what to do with me showing up. I reached a hand out, catching one of hers. "Can you let me be here for you?"

Although this wasn't the moment to have the conversation that needed to be had, the intimacy that flourished so easily between us flickered to life. Luna's eyes softened. She cleared her throat and nodded. "Come in," she said, swinging the door wide. "These are my parents." She gestured toward the couple seated at the kitchen table.

Luna shared her mom's wild curls and her dad's startlingly bright blue eyes.

The tension in her small kitchen was a physical presence. "Mom, Dad, this is Parker. He's my –"

When I sensed her hesitation, I jumped in, "Her boyfriend." I dipped my head in acknowledgment as I studied both of them.

Luna added, "This is Marie and Bill."

Her dad stood from the table and held out his hand. I shook it, taking his measure as I did. His handshake was perfunctory. After he released my hand, he stepped closer to the windows.

Her mom smiled up at me. "I'm sure if you're Jane's boyfriend, you're aware of our life. We were just chatting with Jane about—"

Luna cut in quickly, "Mom, he knows my name is Luna." She clenched her jaw and swallowed. "For God's sake, everyone here calls me Luna because that's my actual name. Please don't call me Jane. It's ridiculous."

Her mother looked legitimately sad for a moment. "I'm sorry, honey, old habits die hard and all that. We still do the RV thing," her mom said, a hint of apology in her tone. "It's a little complicated to get out of that because that's how we make a living."

While I appreciated her honesty about it, the pain radiating from Luna made me angry. Her dad was staying mostly quiet. "Oh, I'm sure that's difficult," I offered vaguely. "Luna has chosen not to do that, so I'm glad you respect her choice."

"Oh, of course, we do!" Her mom rushed in. "But we were just hoping to do a little—"

When she paused, Luna interjected, looking at me as she rolled her eyes. "Content. Do whatever you need to do, but I don't want any part of this."

When I saw motion out of the corner of my eye and noticed her father holding his phone up, I shook my head sharply and crossed over. "Give me your fucking phone. He lifted it high, pulling it away. "This is mine. We have every right to record whatever we want."

"Luna, do you want them recording in your house?" I asked, spinning toward her.

"No, absolutely not," she said quickly.

"Okay, let's go." I reached for her hand, snapping my fingers for Fuzzy to follow.

Her mom hurried to follow us. I stopped by the door, glancing over my shoulder. "This is private property. You actually cannot record without Luna's permission and you definitely cannot record or post this without permission. If you do, trust me, I'll sue you."

Luna's father seemed to have realized this wasn't a great plan and put his phone away. Just as we opened the door, her grandmother was walking onto the porch. "What's going on?" she asked as her eyes bounced among us.

The distress on Luna's face was so obvious that she didn't have to say a word. Her grandmother glared at Luna's parents before turning to smile at me. "You must be Parker."

"Yes, ma'am." I dipped my head. "Nice to meet you. We were just leaving. They want to make content, and Luna wants no part of it."

Luna's grandmother rested both hands on her hips, narrowing her eyes at Luna's parents. "You need to leave. I don't care where you park your RV. If you're gonna pull this shit with her, you cannot be on my property. You absolutely do not have my permission. If you think I won't file a cease and desist order and a restraining order to keep you off this property, think again. You do not have permission to do this."

Luna's mother burst into tears, while her father looked annoyed. Meanwhile, her grandmother continued, "You stole half of her childhood, forcing her to be online all the time. Leave her alone now. I know you love her. You're both better than this.

Why don't you actually try to salvage your relationship with her instead of showing up and trying to
ruin it all over again? At some point, this is going to
have to end." Her grandmother paused, shaking her
head. "Do something else, please."

When I glanced down at Luna, she was swiping
tears off her cheeks. "Are you okay?" I asked under
my breath.

Clearing her throat, she looked up at me and
nodded. "I'm working on it."

"We can still leave," I said.

"I'd like that actually, but give me a minute. I
need to say something to them." She let my hand go
and crossed over to her mother, stopping in front
of her.

We were all gathered at the base of the steps in
front of her small house. "I love you, Mom." She
glanced over to her father. "And, I love you, Dad.
You have to accept I will not be a part of this. At all.
No follow-up reunions on how I'm doing with
strangers online. I respect your choice if you want to
keep doing this, do it, but find a way to do it that
doesn't involve me anymore. It's—" She blinked
away her tears, and my heart twisted in my chest. "I
can't speak for both of you, but I think you're tired
of it. Gram's right. Find something else to do."

"We don't have anywhere to go," her mom said
between sobs.

Luna looked toward her grandmother, who

stepped closer. "You have made enough money to rent a place. Find another option. This isn't her life."

Marie was nodding while her shoulders shook with small sobs. Bill finally snapped out of his annoyance and stepped closer to his wife, curling his arm around her shoulders. "We're gonna figure this out."

Luna opened her mouth to say something, but her grandmother held a hand up. "You can park on my property, not here, but over near my house. Only if you agree to stop this. No filming at all, no content." She looked at Luna's father. "You used to be a handyman. You can do that here. I can't employ both of you, but there are options for you in town. Don't use your daughter and guilt trip her into this. It's not fair."

Luna's mother was nodding along. Her father was harder to read, and I sensed he was wrestling with his pride.

Her grandmother continued, "You'll figure it out. For now, let's move your RV over to park near my place. Are we clear on this? I don't want to hear a peep from Luna that you're pressuring her again."

"You have my word," her father said quietly.

Luna's mom gave her a big hug, squeezing her hands as she stepped away. "I'm sorry. We're just trying to figure this out."

"I know you are," Luna replied.

With her grandmother bossing them along, they

climbed into the RV and drove it to park over near her place. After they were out of sight, her grandmother turned to face me. "I've been wanting to meet you, Parker. I appreciate you standing up for Luna. You be good to her."

"I will. I promise."

"I need to move along and make sure they do what I say." She stopped in front of Luna, reaching for her hands. "Are you okay, hon?"

Luna's tears had dried up. Her smile was a little sad and tired, but it was a smile. "I am. Thank you. You know I worry about them."

"Of course you do. I do too. I think this whole thing spun out of control for them, and they're gonna have to find their way out. I'm sure they're tired, but they will find a different plan. Meanwhile, you let me handle them. You tell me if they try any of that shit."

"You're swearing a lot," Luna teased.

"Well, that's never been off-limits for me. Now, I love you." She leaned over and scratched behind Fuzzy's ears before she walked back down Luna's driveway.

Luna looked up at me, uncertainty flickering in her gaze. "Are we still leaving?"

I didn't know what to say, so I did the only thing I could think to do. I stepped closer to her and wrapped her in my arms. Dipping my head, I rested my chin on her shoulder.

"I fucked up and I'm sorry," I murmured into her hair.

Her reply was muffled against my shoulder. "It's okay."

I loosened my hold. She lifted her head, looking up at me. "What happened?"

I took a shaky breath. "My mom showed up. What are the chances? All the stuff with her, the panic, the abandonment, feeling like I couldn't get it right." I sighed. "I started seeing that therapist. Leo gave me her phone number. You can go to an appointment with me if you want, but I don't have a good reason for being an asshole. It wasn't you. It was all me. I just panicked. Delaney thinks I have old wounds around thinking I'm not worthy because my mom, who was supposed to be there for me, left me. My dad went a long way to helping me repair that, but I still panicked, and I didn't know how to talk about it. I didn't know how to tell you that I didn't feel like I was worthy. I love you. I didn't mean to hurt you. I promise."

Luna held my gaze, not once looking away before she placed her palm in the center of my chest. Her touch was a balm to my unsettled heart. "That makes sense. I guess it's better that this happened now so you could panic and I could deal with my parents, and we could both fuck up at the same time."

I had no idea where Fuzzy had gone, but he suddenly reappeared, circling our legs tightly and then shimmying between us. Luna giggled when she looked down at him. "He's kind of pushy about affection."

"Absolutely." I laughed. "He is. So, do you want me to go? I showed up today because I was going to try to explain and fix it."

"There's nothing more to fix. I'm not perfect, and neither are you. How are things with your mom? What's going on?" she asked softly.

I took a slow breath. "Well, I'm not ready to try to build a relationship with her. Delaney helped me figure out that whatever I feel right now doesn't have to be permanent. I might want to build a connection with her, but not now. That's what I told my mom."

Luna studied me, her gaze warm. "Of course. It's messy, and it'll probably stay that way. Nothing is ever final, not really."

My chest loosened with the tension easing. "I'm sorry I was a coward."

Luna shook her head. "You weren't a coward, Parker. That's a really painful situation, and you were trying to deal with it."

"I feel like I let you down. There's a part of me that worries I can't be good enough for anyone. And, with you, it really matters. I love you."

She stared up at me. "I love you too. I wish you had as much faith in yourself as I have in you." She leaned up and pressed a kiss just below my collar-bone. My heart lunged toward her touch.

"I was coming here today to make it right. Are you okay? I mean…" I thumbed over my shoulder in the general direction of where her parents' RV was now parked.

She rolled her eyes. "I was really stressed out, but honestly, whenever they show up and try to create content and do all that shit, I get really stressed. They know I hate doing it, so they put me on the spot. It sucks." Her lips curled a little at the corners. "Thanks for standing up for me."

"Well, I know you can stand up for yourself, but I was kind of pissed. It was bullshit that your dad whipped his phone out like that."

"That's why they got so popular at first. They didn't even try to edit stuff. After a while, there was only so much to do that felt new. They're not as popular now, so they try to drag me into these re-union things. They were trying to propose a reunion with this other family who has an RV channel. I hate it."

"Your grandma has your back, I have your back, and they're gonna have to figure out something else. They can do the RV thing, but not with you. I mean, if you change your mind…"

Luna laughed, leaning up to press another kiss below my collarbone. The brush of her lips was like fire flickering over my skin. Of course, my body had a mind of its own, and she smiled up at me when it became obvious that I was reacting to her presence. "Ignore it."

"What if I don't want to?" she teased, her voice the crack of a whip.

Chapter Thirty-One

LUNA

As Parker's eyes held mine, I felt held in a beam of love. Maybe I shouldn't have been so quick to let down my guard, but as soon as he explained what he'd been going through, I understood.

This was Parker. This was the guy I'd never forgotten after those few hours of walking on the beach years ago. The guy that saved me while dipnetting. It was just plain easy with him. We had a connection. It felt like kismet.

His brow furrowed with worry. "I don't want you to think I came back just for that. We could go the rest of our lives without that. All I want is to be with you."

I rocked my hips into his before sliding my hand down his chest to stroke over his lengthening arousal.

"Luna," he bit out, his breath hissing through his teeth.

"Parker," I teased, feeling sultry and sly. "I missed you."

"I missed you, but—" Pausing, he gulped in air.

I forced myself to be serious and slid my palm back up over his heart, where I could feel the rapid kick of it against my touch. "I missed you, and I really do understand. I was hurt. You're here, and that's amazing, and we can do tarot cards after."

"After?" he prompted, tipping his head to the side.

Biting my lip, I made a quick decision. Stepping back, I caught his hand in mine and led him up the stairs into the house. Fuzzy was hot on our heels and went straight for his water bowl. I tossed one of his favorite chews into the living room. That would keep him occupied.

In a matter of minutes, we were in my bedroom, and I shut the door, turning to face Parker with my hands on my hips. "You owe me," I announced.

The heat in his gaze sent a blaze of heat through me. "Do I?" he teased, finally getting with the program.

My curls bounced with my nod. "Yes! I've never had makeup sex."

Parker chuckled as I began to unbutton my blouse. Seconds later, we were stripping in between kisses and a few stumbles. When we were standing at the foot of my bed, Parker stilled and rasped, "Wait, Luna."

He lifted a hand to palm my cheek. I felt caught in a burning moment with need and desire rushing through me. For a few seconds, Parker's touch anchored me, centered me in this connection with him. "I love you, Luna, and I always will."

My heart felt connected to his through shimmering strands of love and need and fierce desire. "I love you," I whispered just before he claimed my mouth.

As it always was with him, he kindled the fire inside of me. It felt as if sparks were leaping over my skin when his palm slid down over my belly. I savored his weight as he came over me, stretching my arms over my head. I was lost in his gaze when he shifted closer, notching his crown at my entrance.

My breath was coming in heaves. My skin was burning up for him, and all I wanted was to be as close as we possibly could be. "Hurry, Parker," I gasped.

Locked in the fire of his gaze, I cried out when he filled me with a deep thrust. He held still, brushing my tangled hair away from my face with one hand and his fingers lacing with mine with the other, his grip strong and sure.

"I missed you," he whispered, his voice gruff. "So much."

"You're here now, and that's all that matters. You're right here."

His lips curled slightly at the corners. On the heels of a breath, he filled me. We rocked into each other, and everything spiraled. It felt as if we were spinning together in a net of sparks. My release was barreling toward me as the waves crashed, each rising higher to a crescendo until it broke. I was trembling from the force of it as he reached between us, teasing his fingers exactly where I needed them. Then, it all started breaking apart. I distantly heard him crying my name as he shuddered with me. I felt the heat of his release filling me before he rolled us over together, and I collapsed against his side.

I loved the way he held me close, the feel of his fingers sifting through my tangled curls, and his strong, warm presence beside me.

After a few minutes, we heard the click of Fuzzy's claws on the floor outside the door. Parker's laugh rumbled against my chest. "Someone has expectations," he teased.

When I rose up on one elbow to look at him, I leaned down to give him a quick kiss. "Let's go."

"You're always so energetic after sex," he replied with a chuckle when I bounced up.

I tossed a grin over my shoulder. "I am."

A few minutes later, Parker had followed me downstairs after we both tugged on some clothes.

He went to take Fuzzy for another bathroom break while I checked in the fridge to see what we had for food options. It was still early, but I was starving. My parents had arrived when I normally would've been eating lunch. My refrigerator didn't have much to offer.

When Parker came back in, I glanced over and pointed at the kitchen table. He walked over and looked down at the single tarot card I pulled—the hierophant card.

He glanced at it, his gaze sober as he brought his eyes to mind again. "You know I want to marry you, right?"

"What?" I sputtered.

"Just thought I'd get that out of the way." His lips quirked at the corners. "You do not need to tell me if that's what you want, but that's how I feel."

"Oh, my God," I whispered, letting the refrigerator door close. I breathed, pressing my palm to my chest, trying to calm my racing heartbeat. "Are you serious?"

"Very. That day when we met at the beach? I've never felt like that with anyone. I'm not an idiot. I know being together long-term isn't easy. Hell, I just chickened out on facing you over –"

When he stopped abruptly, I cut in, "Something intense and powerful that you had to face. You're going to keep facing what happened, and it's going to be okay."

My own baggage was messy, but when it came to others, I could see things more clearly.

He swallowed and nodded. "I don't always know how to feel about things, but I know how I feel about you."

I took in a breath and crossed over to him. "Well, I want to marry you too. You're not really asking, so I'm not sure what we're doing here."

Parker's laugh rumbled in his throat. He reached for my hand before leaning forward to give me a fierce kiss. "We're doing things the way we do them. We're gonna get married. We'll figure out the details later."

"What made you say that right now?" I asked.

He gestured to the card. "That means commitment, right?"

"That's one of the meanings." I was still reeling from that. I just drew one from the card deck.

"It reminded me I might as well say what matters right now," he continued. "We can get through the hard stuff together. I love you, Luna."

I blinked away the tears stinging my eyes. "I love you."

Fuzzy came barging in because that's what Fuzzy did. We gave him a little love and laughed.

Chapter Thirty-Two

PARKER

A month later

My dad gave me a bear hug, clapping me on the back the way he always did, hard enough to knock the breath out of me. He stepped back. "I'm so glad you were here for our visit."

My lips curled into a smile. "I'm glad too, Dad. You got to meet Luna."

His gaze swung to Luna who stood beside me talking with Stella's mom.

"You make the best donuts I've ever had," my dad enthused.

Luna's cheeks turned a little pink when she smiled over at him. "I appreciate that. It's really good to meet you."

"You can come visit us anytime, but we're

looking into a move here." My dad lifted his hands up in the air. "Stella is here, you're here, and now you're getting married soon. I mean, if you have kids, we wanna be close to spoil our grandkids."

As I held my dad's eyes, my chest felt tight with emotion. He'd always been somewhat over-enthusiastic with affection. He was still that way, and I loved that about him.

"We'd love that," Luna said.

"Well, we're looking into options. We don't own a house in Fireweed Harbor, so as soon as our lease is up, if we can find something here, we'll move. We're gonna figure it out." He smiled at Elaine. "But we have a ferry to catch, so we gotta go."

There were hugs all around before they drove away in their rental car.

"I'm really glad I got to meet your dad and your stepmom." Luna smiled up at me.

"I am too." That emotion tightened again. It was surprising for me to care about someone meeting my dad, but Luna meant so much. "The timing for their visit was good. I'm probably gonna have to head out soon to that fire up near Fairbanks. Our crew is on rotation."

Luna nodded. "I know. I may never love you traveling, but I know it's part of your job, and you love it."

I dusted a kiss on her cheek. When I lifted my

head, she added, "I need to pop back inside to check with Janet about a few things. Do you want to come with me?"

"Absolutely." It was still pretty early in the morning. "I can always have more coffee," I pointed out with a grin.

Luna squeezed my hand as we walked into the cafe together. Janet was busy checking on something in the oven in the back. "I'm so glad you're here!" she exclaimed the minute her eyes clapped on Luna.

"Yeah? I'm always glad to see you, but what are you so excited about?" Luna asked.

"I think I messed up a batch of donuts. And we're already out," Janet offered with a sheepish smile.

Luna shrugged. "There's always extra dough in the refrigerator." She quickly got to work, and Casey came in the back to hand me a coffee.

In the month since my mom had shown up and Luna's parents had returned in their RV, Luna and I had settled into a rhythm. Janet was busy finalizing the timeline for when Luna would take over the café. Luna was already doing all the baking there and planned to start managing it within the next month, but Janet would keep ownership for five years, or less, until Luna felt ready to fully take over. My mom had left town. She had my phone number, and I had hers, but for now, that was it.

Luna's parents had shocked Luna because they decided to stay in town. She'd initially guessed they'd change their mind and start traveling again. Her dad had taken a small construction job with a business in the area, and her mother was actually working at the local pharmacy. They'd even done a final video for their channel, simply sharing they would update if anything changed for them, but they were taking a break.

As for Luna and me, I was staying with her every night.

"This coffee is perfect." I gave a thumbs up to Casey.

She grinned over at me. "I know your favorite," she teased.

Luna moved at lightning speed, shaping the donuts and checking on another batch of dough that was rising.

Janet caught my eye where I waited with my hips resting on the edge of a stool across from Luna. Janet was getting a tray of baked goods to carry up to the front. "You seem like a happy man, Parker." Her tone was light.

I did a mental body check before a slow smile stretched at the corners of my lips. "I am a happy man."

A little while later, Luna and I walked out of the café. Her hand was warm in mine. When I looked down at her, a feeling that was linked solely to her gusted through me like a warm breeze. A sense of comfort laced with strands of joy.

I stopped her when we reached my truck. "What is it?" she asked.

I dipped my head and gave her a lingering kiss. "What if we went ahead and got married?"

Chapter Thirty-Three

LUNA

A few weeks later

A sense of giddiness washed through me as I looked up at Parker. "I can't believe we did this!"

His slow smile sent my belly spinning. "I can."

I tipped my head to the side as I savored the warmth of his hands holding mine. "And, you were the cynical one."

He waggled his brows. "I was and I still am. A little bit, but you are exempt from my cynicism."

When I giggled, he caught the sound with a kiss.

"Okay, lovebirds, we have food to eat," Beck's voice reached us.

We broke apart, and Parker grinned as he released one of my hands and swung his arm toward the table of food by the wall. "Go for it. You don't have to wait for us."

Beck needed no further invitation and promptly walked over and started serving himself, while Maisie caught my eyes and rolled hers. "He's basically a puppy sometimes."

Hudson stopped beside Parker and pulled him into a backslapping hug while more of our friends surrounded us. This had been a hastily arranged wedding. Janet served as our justice of the peace. We had the ceremony outside the new winery with a stunning backdrop view. We'd said our vows on this cold, early winter afternoon.

Tish stopped beside me to give me a quick hug. When she stepped back, her smile was warm. "I'm so happy for you." Someone called her name. "I'll find you again. I'm going to check to make sure we're on schedule with the food for your reception." She managed the admin part of Fireweed Industries here in Willow Brook.

"Tish, you don't work here. You work at the office," I protested. She shrugged. "I know, but I kind of manage all of the local stuff here. It's your wedding; you're my friend, and I want everything to be perfect." She waved as she hurried off.

My gaze drifted around the room, my eyes landing on my grandmother, who was talking with Janet. Parker was in conversation with Hudson and a cluster of firefighters, so I squeezed his hand before I crossed the room to check in with my grandmother and Janet.

"Thank you, Janet," I said when I stopped in front of her.

"For what?" Her eyes twinkled with her smile.

"Marrying us, setting me up with the donuts and lining things out for me over the next few years for when I take over the café. All of it," I said with feeling. Tears sprung to my eyes as I looked at her.

Janet pulled me into a hug, her embrace warm and comforting. When she stepped back, I added, "Everything feels right, and I'm so grateful to you." I looked down at my grandmother, who was sitting in a chair. "Thank you, Gram. For everything."

She curled an arm around my waist and squeezed. "No need to thank me. This is the way it was supposed to work out."

My parents were here, and I was grateful they were. Something I hadn't been sure I'd have felt at one point. We could never erase those years of content creation, but they'd been true to their word and hadn't once tried to persuade me to take part in a video after that one afternoon. They were both busy with work, and it looked like it was going to work out for them to stay here. They were still living in their RV, but my dad was planning to build something for them on the back of Gram's property.

My gaze arced about the space, and I took a slow breath as that now-familiar sense of giddy joy rose inside when I saw Parker approaching me with a plate from the table.

"What is it?" he asked when he stopped in front of me.

"We did it." Tears wicked up from my heart.

"Are you about to cry?" His eyes widened with worry as he set the plate on a table beside us.

"Happy tears, I promise."

He slipped his arms around my waist. For that moment, it felt like we were all alone in the world, even though we were surrounded by friends and family. "I love you, Luna. I'm really glad you jumped into the "what-if" with me."

I smiled up at him. "That was kind of an easy question."

After a lingering kiss, we enjoyed celebrating our commitment with our friends and family. That night, when we got home, we took Fuzzy for his evening walk. Everything felt just right. We went to our favorite viewing spot on the trail nearby.

Parker looked down at me. "It was only ever you, Luna."

EPILOGUE

Kincaid Greene

"Hey, man." Hudson clapped me on the shoulder as he stopped beside me. "Want a beer? It's open bar," he added with a brow waggle.

A chuckle rustled in my throat. "Crazy, really."

"It's not like Fireweed Industries doesn't have money to waste," he pointed out. "So far, they only had a soft launch for this place. This is the official opening," he pointed out.

"I even heard of Fireweed Winery & Brewery in Minnesota. It's a national name," I replied.

"It's the biggest name in Alaska when it comes to any kind of corporation. They were ahead of the curve when it came to the whole craft beers and wine thing. Anyway, how are you liking it here so far?" he asked.

I paused before nodding. "Love it. I'm used to

long winters, so I'm not worried about that. It's damn pretty country too."

Just then, Parker Reeves approached.

"Ah, here's the man of honor," Hudson said.

Parker, another firefighter on the hotshot crew I'd taken a position with recently, paused beside us, looking bemused. "You don't need to overdo it," he teased. This event was to honor Parker and his fiancée, Luna.

"Dude, you have a love story for the ages," Beck Steele commented as he stopped beside our group.

I'd quickly discovered Beck, a firefighter on another crew in town, was deeply in love with his wife and totally into everyone else being in love.

"For the ages?" I prompted.

Beck nodded, his gaze sobering. "Totally, man. They met one day when they were both in high school, walked on the beach and kissed. And, here we are now. How much later?" He paused, glancing toward Parker.

Parker's lips curled in a bemused smile before adding, "It's been a little over a decade."

"And, you didn't even know her name back then," Beck added.

Parker chuckled. "I do now."

"It was fate," Beck said, his voice full of teasing conviction. He swung his attention to me. "What about you, Kincaid?"

"What about me?" I countered.

"I know you're new to the area and from Minnesota, so you can totally handle winter here. But what's your status? Girlfriend? Wife? Boyfriend? Husband?"

A laugh slipped out. "Uh, none of the above."

"What brought you here?" Beck asked.

"On my mom's bucket list to live here again."

"Really?" Hudson chimed in.

"Yep. She was in the Coast Guard when she was younger and stationed nearby. She always wanted to come back. So here we are."

"You are a good son." Beck's normally teasing gaze was somber.

"Well, I try," I offered with a light shrug.

"How's your mom doing?" he asked.

"Uh..." I paused, because that was a loaded question. She was okay, but she had lupus and was dealing with a cluster of medical complications as a result. But that was a conversation for another day. "She's good," I said simply. She was in spirit, and that was really all that mattered.

"Excellent. Well, when you meet, I don't know, the man or woman of your dreams, let me know. I'll give you all the advice you need," Beck said.

Parker rolled his eyes, hard. "You know, Beck, you're not the only guy here who's a family man and happy about it."

"Beck's the office gossip, always in everybody's business," Hudson interjected dryly.

Luna approached, and Parker immediately curled his arm around her shoulders, snugging her against his side. He leaned close to give her a lingering kiss. The love between them practically shimmered in the air around them.

I wasn't prone to being a corny, romantic guy, but in this moment, there was no doubt these two were happy together.

Conversation floated around us with congratulations to Parker and Luna punctuating many comments. The event in question had been thrown by the fire station, the crews all pitching in together with a big assist from Fireweed Winery because they were having their grand opening and thought it would be perfect to celebrate a couple's engagement.

I loved Willow Brook and Alaska so far. I was even more pleased to be on the crew. When you're a hotshot firefighter, you learn there's a certain mindset required. It takes a lot of nerve and a lot of confidence, and sometimes that could translate into arrogance, which wasn't healthy for the work. The tone set here didn't brook that kind of attitude. Everyone had each other's backs, and I liked it.

I still wondered if my mother's hopes for our move to Alaska would ever come to fruition. But that was also a topic for another day, or rather, a question. One that had feathered in the back of my thoughts for most of my life.

"Hi guys," a voice said, and I glanced over, my

gaze locking with a stunning pair of hazel eyes set off by glossy dark bangs framing the waitress's pretty face.

It wasn't as if I hadn't seen a beautiful woman before, but this one elicited a startling jolt. My thoughts swirled with curiosity, but all she was doing was checking to see if we needed any drinks.

TORI SHACKLEFORD

The pace that evening at work was busy on steroids. For the most part, the eddy of customers flowed around me like an orchestra. Until one moment. I was stunned into silence when I locked eyes with a man, one I'd never seen before. Shaggy, honey-brown hair, rich cognac eyes.

Of course he was a firefighter. There were a sur-plus of them here in Willow Brook.

I wanted to know his name, but I was working. When I hurried by him later, he caught my eye again and his lips quirked at the corners. My belly re-sponded with a spinning flip followed by a shimmy.

———

A few days later

· · ·

I sat down on a large boulder, letting out a happy sigh. It was just me, myself, and my ancient dog, Bella. She promptly began sniffing everything she could, every grain of sand, every rock, pieces of seaweed, the ocean water lapping at the sand, the air, all of it.

"Home," I said aloud.

Willow Brook was home, along with Alaska and this little spot on the beach here. When I was a little girl, my mom used to take us here for walks, for frolicking, for clam digging, and more.

Looking for a distraction, I leaned down, scooping up a piece of lava rock. These were my favorite rocks. They were lightweight, as if they'd been dropped here from another galaxy. This one was a deep burgundy color on one side that transitioned into black on the other. I lightly tossed it back and forth in my hands before setting it down on the boulder, planning to take it home with me.

I sat on that boulder for a little while, savoring the salty air and the birds chattering above the shoreline before I called Bella back. She was mostly deaf, but if I managed to make eye contact when I said her name, she came right over. She was a medium-sized brown dog with a half-tail. The vet said something must've happened to her tail, but she didn't know what.

Bella was my shadow, my soul dog. She went everywhere with me and was as loyal as a dog could be. Just as I got in the car, I heard a buzzing sound and glanced over to see some kind of wasp flying straight for me. I yelled and swatted at it, but it zoomed right back and stung me just above my collarbone.

"Asshole!" I pointlessly hollered.

A few minutes later, I was driving back toward Willow Brook, toward home. The last thing I recalled was Bella letting out a sharp, unexpected bark. I woke up to the sound of the tail-end of my own yelp.

"There she is," a rumbling voice said.

I fought through layers of confusion and tried to drag in a deep breath, but my throat felt unbelievably tight. "Take it easy," the voice said. "You're in the middle of an anaphylactic reaction. The antihistamine shot should be taking effect. Give it a few minutes, and you'll be able to breathe a little better."

I dragged my eyes open and looked around wildly. I felt funny all over, and my throat was itchy and scratchy.

"Your dog is a good girl," the man said when I finally managed to focus on his face.

Holy wow. Even though I was half out of it, I knew a handsome man when I saw one. This guy was all handsome. His concerned brown eyes held mine. "How are you doing?"

My mind distantly clocked that I'd seen him at work the other night. He seemed professional. He was kneeling in the open driver's side door of my car with what appeared to be a bag with medical supplies on the ground.

"Did I pass out while I was driving?" I took another breath and discovered the tightness was loosening in my throat. I got more oxygen this time, and the fog in my brain started to clear.

Bella was beside me, her chin on my thigh. "I'm guessing you got stung by something." He lightly tapped his fingertip right where that stupid wasp, or whatever, had stung me.

"Yeah, right before I got in my car. I've been stung before," I said slowly, as my thoughts started to organize themselves a little more coherently.

"Most people don't have a reaction until their second sting," he said. "You slid off the road and your dog here started barking up a storm. I had my windows down nearby and heard her."

"Oh," I said brilliantly. "Are you an EMT?" I asked another moment later.

He was tucking things away in his bag. His gaze lifted to mine again. Although, apparently, I had almost just died from anaphylactic shock, my belly did a little swoop when his rich chocolate gaze snagged mine. His shaggy brown hair fell over his eyes. He had a straight nose, strong cheekbones that angled down to molded lips, and a square jaw with a little dimple at the base of his chin.

His lips kicked up at one corner and, holy hell,

another dimple peaked out. "I'm a hotshot firefighter, not officially an EMT, but we all have first responder training, kinda part of the job."

My lips still felt a little funny, and I pressed them together quickly, relieved that the numbness and tingling were starting to wear off. "You can't throw a rock in Willow Brook without hitting a hotshot," I managed to tease.

He chuckled, and the sound spun through me, turning my belly in another dizzying flip. "True," he said as he tipped his head to the side.

He leaned back, and I was abruptly disappointed to have him move away from me. "Are you leaving now?" Alarm shot through me with dizzying anxiety on its heels. I had just passed out in my car by myself with my dog.

"I'm not leaving," he replied, his tone easygoing. "You shouldn't drive for a while. Also, when you drove off the road, you collided with a boulder."

"What?" I shook my head, trying to think. "Is my car okay?"

"Mostly. You have a small dent in your bumper, but you also have a flat tire and a bent rim. I'll give you a ride. To be on the safe side, we should probably take you to the hospital to get you checked out."

"Oh, no, no, no." I waved a hand, the motion wobbly. "I'm fine, right? You gave me a shot, and I'm all set," I protested.

"Am I gonna have to be official and insist?" He looked genuinely concerned, his gorgeous brown eyes studying me.

I let out a sigh. "No, I'll go." Bella nudged my knee with her nose, and I absently stroked her head.

Eventually, he helped me out of the car. It was not a bad deal to have his strong hands guiding me up and out. He kept an arm around my shoulders to help me walk up the slight incline to his truck.

Bella was practically glued to my calves. He insisted on lifting me into his passenger seat and buckling me in. Maybe it was because I was a little out of it, but when he leaned over to buckle my seatbelt, I almost kissed him.

Once I was situated, he opened the back door and lifted Bella into the back. She immediately poked her head in between the seats and licked my elbow.

He chuckled. "She takes good care of you."

"Bella is my family," I said simply as I leaned over and gave her a kiss on top of her head.

His lips quirked at the corners. "Good to know her name."

I tried to carry on a conversation on the drive to the hospital, but I was still hazy. I learned his name was Kincaid. He'd recently moved to Willow Brook when he accepted a position on one of the hotshot crews here. He was from somewhere in the lower 48, but I couldn't remember where.

We got into a little standoff at the hospital when he wanted to put me in a wheelchair and wheel me in. I refused. "No."

When his lips twitched at the corners, I felt all tingly inside.

Without a word, he curled around my waist and walked me inside. When we stopped in front of the circular desk, a familiar face looked up at me. "Tori!"

"Holly?"

Holly grinned. "I heard you were back in town and that you've been working at Fireweed Winery, but I haven't seen you." Her eyes shifted to Kincaid. "Is she okay?"

Thank you for reading Luna & Parker's story! Want a glimpse of the future for them? Join my newsletter to receive an exclusive scene.

Sign up here: https://BookHip.com/CHJHMMJ

p.s. If you are already subscribed, you'll still be able to access the scene.

Up next is in the Wild Fire Series is Just For Us.

When a bee sting sends me crashing into a boulder,

hotshot firefighter Kincaid Greene comes to my rescue — all smoldering with firefighter hero vibes.

I've sworn off love, but Kincaid doesn't seem to care. One kiss, one chance, and suddenly my heart's in freefall.

Too bad falling for him feels like playing with fire... and I might just get burned.

One-click: Just For Us due out spring 2026!

For more swoon & sass...

This Crazy Love kicks off the Swoon Series - small town southern romance with enough heat to melt you! Jackson & Shay's story is epic - swoon-worthy & intensely emotional. Jackson just happens to be Shay's brother's best friend. He's also *seriously* easy on the eyes. Shay has a past, the kind of past she would most definitely like to forget. Past or not, Jackson is about to rock her world. Don't miss their story!

Burn For Me is a second chance romance for the ages. Sexy firefighters? Check. Rugged men? Check. Wrapped up together? Check. Brave the fire in this hot, small-town romance. Amelia & Cade were high school sweethearts & then it all fell apart. When they cross paths again, it's epic - don't miss Cade's story!

For more small town romance, take a visit to Last Frontier Lodge in Diamond Creek. A sexy, alpha SEAL meets his match with a brainy heroine in Take Me Home. Marley is all brains & Gage is all brawn. Sparks fly when their worlds collide. Don't miss Gage & Marley's story!

If sports romance lights your spark, check out The Play. Liam is a British footballer who falls for Olivia, his doctor. A twist of forbidden heats up this swoon-worthy & laugh-out-loud romance. Don't miss Liam & Olivia's story.

Be sure to sign up for my newsletter for the latest news, teasers & more! Click here to sign up: http://jhcroixauthor.com/subscribe/

FIND MY BOOKS

Thank you for reading Only Ever You! I hope you enjoyed the story. If so, you can help other readers find my books in a variety of ways.

1) Write a review!
2) Sign up for my newsletter, so you can receive information about upcoming new releases & receive a FREE copy of one of my books: http://jhcroixauthor.com/subscribe/
3) Like and follow my Amazon Author page at https://amazon.com/author/jhcroix
4) Follow me on Bookbub at https://www.bookbub.com/authors/j-h-croix
5) Follow me on Instagram at https://www.instagram.com/jhcroix/

6) Like my Facebook page at https://www.facebook.com/jhcroix

Wild Fire Series
  All The Afters
  When We Dare
  Fake It True
  Only Ever You
  Just For Us - due out 2026
  Heartfire Falls Series
  What We Keep
  Mine To Hold - due out early 2026!
  Fireweed Harbor Series
  Make You Mine
  Dare To Fall
  Be The One
  One More Time
  Wait For You
  Ever After All
  Light My Fire Series
  Wild With You
  Hold Me Now
  Only Ever Us
  Fall For Me
  Keep Me Close
  With Every Breath
  All It Takes

Take Me Now
Meant To Be
Dare With Me Series
Crash Into You
Evers & Afters
Come To Me
Back To Us
Take Me There
After We Fall
Swoon Series
This Crazy Love
Wait For Me
Break My Fall
Truly Madly Mine
Still Go Crazy
If We Dare
Steal My Heart
Into The Fire Series
Burn For Me
Slow Burn
Burn So Bad
Hot Mess
Burn So Good
Sweet Fire
Play With Fire
Melt With You
Burn For You
Crash & Burn
That Snowy Night

Haven's Bay Holiday Series
All I Want
All I Need
All We Have
All We Are
Brit Boys Sports Romance
The Play
Big Win
Out Of Bounds
Play Me
Naughty Wish
Diamond Creek Alaska Novels
When Love Comes
Follow Love
Love Unbroken
Love Untamed
Tumble Into Love
Christmas Nights
Lodge Series
Take Me Home
Love at Last
Just This Once
Falling Fast
Stay With Me
When We Fall
Hold Me Close
Crazy For You
Just Us

ACKNOWLEDGMENTS

If you're here, you read the whole book! I hope. There aren't enough ways to thank my readers. Thank you anyway - for taking a chance on my stories if this is your first one, or following along if you've read my stories before.

Gracious thanks to Virginia Tesi Carey for editing Luna and Parker's story. More thanks to Terri D. for proofreading and scouring the words to find pesky errors. As always, I'm deeply grateful to my early readers who let me know about any stubborn mistakes.

Much gratitude to Najla Qamber for yet another gorgeous cover. My assistant, Erin, handles so many details on the back-end for me and manages to make it look like I might be sort of organized. Thanks to my publicist, Dani Sanchez, for guiding me along the way and helping me get over it already when it comes to actually announcing my books to the world.

To my sweet dogs, who alternate between

watching the birds, accompanying me on morning runs, and napping beside me when I write. To my family, for always being there.

xoxo
J.H. Croix

ABOUT THE AUTHOR

USA Today Bestselling Author J. H. Croix lives in a small town with her husband and two spoiled dogs. Croix writes contemporary romance with sassy women and alpha men who aren't afraid to show some emotion. Croix's love for quirky small towns runs deep and includes living in Alaska in a tiny coastal town for over a decade. Her love for these special places and the characters that inhabit them shines through in her writing. When she's not writing, you can find her cooking, counting the birds in her backyard, and running with her dogs, which is when her best plotting happens.

Places you can find me:
jhcroixauthor.com

facebook.com/jhcroix

instagram.com/jhcroix

bookbub.com/authors/j-h-croix